Get Your
Coventry Romances
Home Subscription NOW

And Get These
4 Best-Selling Novels
FREE:

LACEY
by Claudette Williams

THE ROMANTIC WIDOW
by Mollie Chappell

HELENE
by Leonora Blythe

THE HEARTBREAK TRIANGLE
by Nora Hampton

CATHERINE

by

Audrey Blanshard

FAWCETT COVENTRY • NEW YORK

CATHERINE

This book contains the complete text of the original hardcover edition.

Published by Fawcett Coventry Books, a unit of CBS Publications, the Consumer Publishing Division of CBS Inc., by arrangement with Robert Hale Limited

ISBN: 0-449-50189-2

Printed in the United States of America

First Fawcett Coventry printing: June 1981

10 9 8 7 6 5 4 3 2 1

CATHERINE

ONE

"There, Cathy!" Mrs Wilby laid a lilac-gloved hand gently on the sleeve of the young lady walking by her side. "I do believe—yes—that is the *Princess herself* approaching!"

Miss Ebford halted at once under her companion's touch. They were walking through Cockspur Street, and nearing the end of the cul-de-sac in which stood Warwick House, the dingy and neglected London home of the Princess Charlotte; so there was no need to elaborate as to which member of the royal family was meant. A carriage, of no particular splendour, was drawn up in the roadway ahead, but its door was held open by a footman whose livery had caught Mrs Wilby's knowledgeable eye. In any event, as far as Catherine was concerned, Charlotte was the only one of all the fairly numerous princesses who signified to her:

she felt an especial bond with Her Highness, for they shared the same natal day—January 7th 1796—and had celebrated their eighteenth birthday six months before. Catherine had for many years followed the fortunes of this exalted personage through the pages of the magazines and prints, whose formal reports were, of course, constantly embellished for her by hearsay; and there was no lack of *on dits* at the moment due to the recent announcement of her betrothal to the Prince of Orange.

This was Catherine's first actual sight of 'her' Princess, and by now she naturally held certain preconceived notions as to her appearance. Looking for an elegant, tastefully-dressed, dignified and, above all—since her engagement—a radiant girl, she had to own to a certain dismay over the hoydenish creature who now bounded gracelessly out of the side street and into her carriage, revealing as she did so a quite shocking degree of ankle. Her pelisse, too, would certainly be described as gaudy by Catherine's guide and mentor, Lady Olivia Dauntry. And, finally, the slightly protuberant eyes held no radiance in the pale face, only a hint of *tristesse*, or—could it be?—ill-temper.

A lady-in-waiting followed her mistress at a distinctly more regal pace, acknowledging their disregarded curtsies with a faint, suffering smile. After the Princess had been driven off with her, they continued on their own way in the direction of the Strand and, more particularly, Ebford's, the banking house owned by Catherine's guardian.

Honora Wilby, who had sometimes in the past seen the Princess Charlotte's mother, the buxom and over-dressed Princess of Wales (her painted eyebrows had been distressingly manifest at five yards distance), was less disappointed than Catherine by her latest glimpse of royalty. "A fine figure the girl has, and, you know, there is a great deal of intelligence in the countenance," she said judiciously, breaking the stunned silence of her fellow witness.

Catherine agreed, but felt she could not but remark upon the positively sulky expression marring the intelligent royal face that day.

"True: and the Princess is noted, I collect, for her gaiety and liveliness." Mrs Wilby lowered her rather weak voice still further, although there was scant danger of being overheard in the noisy street: "It's my belief she is not feeling in good point—mark my words."

Catherine cast the unassuming and diffident lady whom she called Aunt a look of alarm; for if there was one faculty of which Aunt Wilby was confident, it was her uncanny knack of detecting threatening symptoms in others. "Don't say she is sinking into a decline—and just before her marriage!" But that was a trifle hard to believe, she told herself, recalling that above-all exuberant progress from house to carriage.

Mrs Wilby pursed her lips and shook her head bodingly. "*Because* of this wedding, more like," she murmured almost to herself; so that Catherine, an inch or two taller than she, barely caught the doom-laden comment.

"Oh, come now, Aunt!"

Startled by her own temerity in making animadversions upon royalty, Mrs Wilby at once sought to retract. "No, I daresay it is in no way connected—not but what there has been *much talk* about the continuing absence of a fixed date for the ceremony. But there again, there must be so many difficulties to surmount in such an affair," she vacillated once more.

Catherine had not really been paying attention to this exchange, and as they approached Charing Cross she ceased listening altogether and drifted off into her own thoughts. She had once cherished a secret dream that she might share a wedding date with the Princess as well as just a birthday: it was sheer foolishness, of course, and now, however much the royal ceremony was put off it was scarcely likely she could achieve her odd ambition now.

But then, it didn't matter a groat when she married as long as she made the right choice, she reflected cheerfully. That she would be allowed to choose a partner she was in no doubt: her guardian, Lord Ebford, had always taken scant interest in her matrimonial future. He was wholly absorbed in his banking; and, since her younger brother Benjamin had sadly frustrated all the Baron's hopes for his future in the Bank by running away to sea after only two weeks spent there, it would not be wonderful if he should tend to wash his hands of her own welfare. At Miss Jamieson's Seminary, where she had been a parlour-boarder until only six months before, two of her friends had faced the prospect of arranged marriages, and she had marvelled at their acquiescence. She would never be told where she must marry, she had always maintained—and meant it. Perhaps being a foundling had something to do with her attitude. After all, she conceded, it might be different if two ancient houses wished their illustrious offspring to unite for some particular reason of their own. Even so, she was not at all sure she would wed merely to oblige her family, whatever the circumstances.

The truth was that in spite of being a foundling she had always been an independent miss (Miss Jamieson's own description on many occasions); and the expensive schooling had strengthened for confidence in her self and effectively divorced her from any feeling of family ties with her guardian and Aunt Wilby—who was not her real aunt, merely a distant cousin of Lord Ebord's wife. When Lady Ebford had died, and Cathy now retained only the haziest memory of her, being only six years old at the time, the fortuitously widowed Honora Wilby had been summoned to London from her snug Brighthelmstone villa to take charge of the two young adopted children she had never seen.

But it had not taken long for it to become apparent that Mrs Wilby was quite unequal to the task before her, and Lord Ebford had put both of the children to school as soon as they reached the age of eight. Catherine had disliked her schooldays in the beginning, but as the years went by school became more of a home to her than his lordship's ever-changing London residences. She had invariably looked forward with great eagerness, though, to seeing Benjamin in the holidays; he was, after all, the only true relation she had in the world. Unfortunately his own streak of sturdy independence was stronger even than hers; he had run away from school on two occasions, and then finally absconded from the Bank.

Catherine sighed, as she often did these days

when she thought of Ben. It was fully a year since he had sailed away, and not one word had been heard of him since.

They were now passing Drummonds Bank, and Mrs Wilby, misinterpreting Catherine's show of discontent, remarked: "Yes, it is galling, is it not, to see such a throng of carriages outside the Scotch Bank. Did I tell you, I saw the Duke of Cumberland being escorted to his equipage by Mr Andrew Drummond himself once?—poor Ebford, if only he could achieve Royal Patronage!" And she gave a deep regretful sigh herself.

Catherine was amused that her aunt should think her as passionately concerned in the fortunes of the Bank as she seemed to be herself. Aunt Wilby even used Lord Ebford's own derogatory name for Drummonds, she noticed. For her own part she was happy to look in at Ebfords and see her stepfather (as she had always called him) as often as he should wish it, but she was perfectly sure he did not expect her to inquire into the Bank's affairs at the same time. Indeed, he had not once adverted to business matters with her directly. This was not to say she was a complete ignoramus upon the subject; Aunt Wilby often disclosed titbits to her. "Perhaps all those carriage people are there to demand immense loans which they cannot ever repay, and the Drummonds will be ruined within the year!" she suggested mischievously.

"Pray don't jest, my dear, upon such serious things!" came the quite shocked reply. "Besides, the Scotch Bankers would never be so foolish—not like some I could name."

"Not step-papa, surely?"

"No, of course not . . . but I have said more than I should already."

There was little need to say more, thought Catherine, for Mr William Dauntry was Lord Ebford's partner and the only other possible candidate for her aunt's censure. She hoped Mr Dauntry was not going to cause the Bank to fail; not entirely because of the financial discomfort such an event would be bound to inflict upon them all, but chiefly because his family were particular friends of hers and the severing of that connexion would give her great pain. Lady Olivia, his wife, had taken Catherine under her wing these past four years, and only recently had chaperoned her to all the more tonnish gatherings. Mrs Wilby had gladly relinquished her responsibility on these occasions, bowing to her ladyship's superiority in the role due to her position in Society. Melissa, Lady Olivia's daughter, had shared two years at the same seminary with Cathy, and they had formed a fairly close bond of friendship due to that circumstance. Then there was Christopher, the Dauntrys' only son, who, Cathy suspected sometimes, might be nursing a *tendre* for her. He was just down from Cambridge and there was some expectation that he would join his father at Ebford's with a view to becoming a partner himself one day; but not if his parent had ruined them in the meanwhile, she thought with further disquiet.

If Catherine were completely honest with herself, she had to own that the possibility of seeing Christopher at the Bank was the real reason she was so compliant about these frequent visits to an otherwise monstrously dreary place.

13

She was not to be disappointed that afternoon. It was a warm sunny day and the doors were propped open, and as the uniformed porter greeted them with the customary low bow she immediately caught a glimpse of the familiar slim back. She noticed he was wearing the olive green coat with velvet collar which so suited his auburn colouring. He was with his father, nodding his head occasionally in agreement, but Mr Dauntry senior glimpsed their arrival over his son's shoulder and stepped forward, talking ebulliently all the while.

"How delightful! Yes, indeed! Ebford will be pleased—Rogers!" He snapped his pudgy fingers, but the clerk was already on hand to take the visitors into the special parlour reserved for visits from the founder's relations and personal friends.

Mr William Dauntry was a plump middle-aged person with a moon face, which constantly displayed a row of sound but yellowish teeth: he was an indefatigable talker and an even more persistent smiler. Whatever the subject under discussion his countenance beamed with the steadiest good humour. Indeed, the only modification Cathy had ever witnessed—when he was condoling with a bereaved client—was the solemn shrouding of those teeth with his lips, which merely rendered the grin into a smirk. She thought that perhaps if his features were rubicund and florid, as befitted such an inexhaustible flow of spirits, the effect would be more comfortable; as it was, his complexion was as jaundiced as his teeth.

Having urgently summoned Rogers, Mr Dauntry then proceeded to detain the ladies with his chatter. "Not such a press of folk in the streets today to obstruct your path, eh, ma'am?" he addressed Mrs Wilby. "Still, it ill behoves us to carp at victory celebrations, I daresay! But I own I shall feel relief when these foreign potentates have quit our midst. Why, when the Prussian fellow and his family arrived there were carriages from here to Deptford! I wouldn't take the risk of bringing in mine, and so had to ride all the way from Portland Street. Of course, you know for yourself how it has been!" He gave a bark of laughter.

Whilst his father spoke to Mrs Wilby in this strain Christopher was gazing fondly at Catherine. After their first words of greeting the two young people were silent. Catherine wished sometimes that Chris was not quite so tongued-tied, although she knew the reason was not far to seek; with such a garrulous parent to contend with it was scarcely surprising that he should be rendered mute when in his company. However, she had discovered that even in the ordinary way he was not exactly loquacious.

In appearance, too, he was the antithesis of his parent. Although there was only an inch or two difference in height, he looked a good deal taller than Mr Dauntry on account of his spare frame. His face also lacked the pudginess of his father's, although some resemblance might be seen in the grey-green eyes and the shape of the nose. But the startling variation lay in Christopher's healthy complexion. In one of her more fanciful moments, when she had first seen father and son side by side, she had thought Mr Dauntry, in the black clothes he usually wore, and with his pallid face and grizzled hair, looked for all the world as if he were a print waiting to be painted: whereas Christopher, clad then in a *Bleu Celeste* coat, pantaloons of pale yellow and with reddish locks framing a glowing countenance, seemed to represent a brightly coloured finished print.

Mr Dauntry, although still talking, had evidently decided at last to consign the ladies into the care of the hovering clerk. "Rogers, conduct Mrs Wilby and Miss Ebford into the little parlour and apprise his lordship of their arrival, if you will."

"Certainly, sir." The clerk then coughed in a discreet manner and ventured: "But is he not presently engaged with an Important Client?"

"Bless my soul, of course he is! Quite slipped my mind! It's Berrington," he told his son in a grinning aside. "The prize plum I was just speaking of. Still, they've been closeted together this hour and more. Ebford will join you soon, depend on it, ma'am."

Mrs Wilby smiled back her complaisance, but knew from long experience how profitless it was to try and speak. And sure enough Mr Dauntry was continuing inexorably: "Rogers, mind that the usual refreshments are sent in to the little parlour, if you will. Now, you must excuse me, ladies—some postings to cast my eye over, you know!" His sudden and unexpected crack of laughter startled a gentleman transacting some business at the counter behind them, to such a degree that he dropped his cane. "Christopher, my boy, I will see you at Portland Place at the customary hour—we aren't promised anywhere tonight, are we? No, else I'm perfectly sure I should have remembered Olivia mentioning it to me," he assured himself benignly.

Then, at long last, Rogers was allowed to usher Mrs Wilby and her charge from the hall into the parlour, which was situated up a single pair of stairs at the rear of the tall, narrow building. While Mr Dauntry had been holding forth Catherine had contrived to ask Christopher in an undertone who was this Mr Berrington, to warrant such lengthy attention from his lordship. He, glad to have something easy to say to her, gave one of his rather sweet smiles—which were as rare as his father's were commonplace—and murmured: "Oh, a very warm man indeed, with government connexions at the highest level which would be a honeyfall for any banker—one worth bartering his very soul for! But Lord Ebford will have to be up to snuff to snatch *that* account from Child's, believe me."

Catherine had to be content with this rather unsatisfying contact with him, for at that point she was carried away by Rogers. She had not been in any way interested in the boring Mr Berrington, but felt that at least the rich client had served her to wring an utterance from Chris, however impersonal.

The small room was sparsely furnished with a table, four upright chairs and a glazed bookcase containing the sort of legal and mercantile tomes which were highly unlikely to distract the visitors' attention from the Thames; just visible through the window.

When the clerk had gone out, Mrs Wilby, whose

figure bordered on the stout, sat down, gave a small groan of relief, and began to loosen the criss-crossed laces of her lilac kid sandals. Catherine meanwhile went to the window and studied the distant river scene: observing the ships brought her brother to mind at once, even more than the Bank did, for she had been away at school during his brief sojourn there. And when a moment later a younger clerk—seventeen or so, of an age with Ben—brought in their refreshments, she was further reminded of him.

"Good-day, Charlie," she said cordially, as he set down the heavy silver tray, which looked incongruous in this bare parlour.

Charlie Bone had been Ben's particular chum for the brief time he had lived in at Ebford's, and was Cathy's only direct source of information concerning her brother's disappearance; for it was not to be expected that he would have confided his plans to Lord Ebford. Indeed, Charlie had kept a letter from Ben for her until such time as he had been able to hand it to her surreptitiously one day while she was here. Not even Aunt Wilby knew of the missive's existence. Unfortunately, after all this contriving, it had left her little wiser than before: beyond telling of his inability to face spending the rest of his days cooped up in the Bank, and feeling it incumbent upon him to quit Lord Ebford's guardianship before further instruction was squandered on him, and beyond grieving that he would not see his dearest Cathy 'for years and years if ever again', all he divulged of his future plans was an avowed intention to sail to America. This scheme had caused his fond sister no small anxiety, for the two countries were still at war and she could only suppose he might have joined the crew of a fighting ship. Ever since, she had read of Atlantic battles with a failing heart, and quite unable to share her fears with anyone.

Whenever she visited the Bank Charlie could not ask outright after Ben, but invariably those bleak blue eyes of his in the under-nourished face were turned upon her in mute inquiry, to which she had to respond with a slight shake of her head; as she did today.

Mrs Wilby, who had now eased her swollen ankles, became vaguely aware of this unspoken communication between the young people. She glanced swiftly from Catherine to Mr Bone; who did indeed seem to be all bone with his knobby wrists protruding from the too-short black sleeves of his old and worn coat. No, it was not to be thought of that these two would make sheeps' eyes at each other, she assured herself: Cathy was destined if not for a Brilliant Alliance precisely, at least for a connexion which would place her in another world from a penniless clerk. The chaperon relaxed, and accepted a glass of her favourite Madeira wine from the boy, whose wide blue gaze was now merely respectful to them both.

Charlie then took over to Catherine her usual glass of lemonade. As he did so, he eyed the drink so covetously that she was tempted to offer it back to him. She had no reason to suppose that Ben had left the Bank because he was starved, but if Charlie's appearance was anything to judge by her guardian was not guilty of over-indulging his clerks. Had they been alone she would not have hesitated to let Charlie drink his fill, but Aunt

Wilby would certainly not have approved and perhaps might let something slip to her noble kinsman.

As it happened it was fortunate that she was thus restrained from kindly intention: Lord Ebford entered just as Mr Bone was about to return, with thirst unslaked, to his duties.

The Banker, tall, lean and in his late fifties, with wavy hair still black but thinning on top, and possessed of penetrating dark eyes (useful, Cathy supposed, for repelling clients of dubious repute and assets), seemed to tower over Charlie as the latter scuttled from the parlour.

"Ah, George—I fancy it is very close in here today: will you not join us in a glass?" Mrs Wilby said, eyeing her relation narrowly as she offered him some of his own refreshments.

Catherine too noticed that her guardian, a man with an exceptionally calm and deliberate mien in the ordinary way, now seemed a trifle agitated. Under the dark, dry skin of his cheeks there were two unfamiliar spots of colour.

"Thank you, no, ma'am," he responded in his clipped fashion. "Catherine—I'd be obliged if you would step into my room for a moment." He held open the door and inclined his head to Mrs Wilby. "We shan't detain you long, Honora."

Lord! thought Catherine, who had never before been privileged to see his Sanctum, and for whom these duty visits were customarily uneventful in the extreme: what was afoot? It must concern Ben, she decided, with a nervous start; his ingrate behaviour being the only circumstance likely in her knowledge to work upon his lordship so powerfully. Perhaps his whereabouts had been discovered at last—perhaps he was even now returned home! Or—heaven forbid—dead. With a somewhat shaky hand she replaced the lemonade untouched upon the salver, hoping it might yet find its way to Mr Bone, and walked with rapid step past her waiting guardian.

TWO

By the time Lord Ebford had led his step-daughter into his room she had already visualized three different and dreadful ends for Ben: namely, death by drowning, fever, or cannon shot.

His lordship drew up a chair before his impressive mahogany desk and invited her to be seated, whilst he settled himself in the high-backed, throne-like seat opposite. Catherine did not dare to raise her eyes and see confirmation of her fears in his; instead she watched his hands as they fussily set to rights the standish and one or two weighty books, and then shuffled into order some papers directly before him.

"Well, now," he said at last, and although she had been waiting for him to speak for a good two minutes, she jumped. He frowned at this nervousness. "Come, I am not such an ogre, am I? That I may stand accused of erring on the side of neglect in regard to your unbringing, I don't deny, but no one, I think, would judge me unduly harsh."

Catherine, annoyed that he should have observed her flinch in that goose-ish fashion, for in the general way she was not afraid of him, merely shook her head, and waited with continuing anxiety for him to come to the point.

But he merely rested back against the red velvet, his hands now gripping the edge of the desk, and surveyed her for another long moment. His gaze travelled slowly from her oval face and neat, well-defined features, framed by shining brown curls and a most stylish bonnet, to her gloved hands folded in her lap. "Yes . . ." he murmured then, "it's my belief that my wife would not be disappointed if she could see you now. You do not want for physical attractions, and Lady Olivia has exceeded herself in dressing you to your best advantage—as I knew she would, else, I shouldn't have chosen her for the task."

She was thoroughly unnerved by the scrutiny of those dark eyes, and the surely prevaricating tenor of the discourse. She stared fixedly at the carved bracket foot of the desk.

"However, I can't so congratulate myself on the handling of your young brother." Bitterness sharpened his voice and he released his grip on the table and slumped forward in an uncharacteristic gesture of despondency. "I daresay you may be critical of me for not pursuing the miscreant, eh, and for not having him brought back safe and sound under my care again?"

In fact she was wholly unaware of his negligence in that affair, as he might have called out all the Runners in London at the time for all she knew, but she could not regard the omission with anything but relief; if Ben wanted his freedom, then so did she for him.

Her step-father did not pause for a reply to his question. "But no one—*no one*—who tosses my charity back after all those years can expect to return as if nothing has occurred. No, I wash my hands of your brother, miss, but it gives me no pleasure to do so, I'll have you know. I took him—as I did you—a homeless orphan: I gave him my own name and was prepared to rear him almost as a—" he hesitated "—son. And that notwithstanding that I do have a son of my own, Catherine. You didn't know that, I collect?"

She was considerably startled, and looked up expecting to meet his hard stare. But the emotionless voice had not prepared her for a face of grief. "No, sir, I had no notion," she murmured gently. Her guardian had always been very remote to her hitherto, and had certainly never spoken in his strain. She had been brought up in the full knowledge that she and Ben were foundlings, their origins completely obscure, and that they owed everything they had to Lord Ebford and his late wife. This was tacitly understood, and until now no overt mention of their position had been made by either his lordship or themselves. To strangers they were always presented as step-children.

"He is a year older than you," the Banker was saying in the same dead voice, "and cannot read or write and never will. Oh, he is well-cared for and, as far as one can ever know, happy enough." He lifted his black-clad shoulders, expressively. "I never talk of it, and try not to think of it—it would serve no purpose. I abandoned hope for him long ago. But you do apprehend why Benjamin's treachery has been particularly hard for me to bear?—I am sure you do," he added in his usual astringent tone. "And no more will ever be said by me on that head."

Catherine was completely shattered by these revelations from him, and, although she would never have condemned Ben to a life of misery in the Bank, she now wished with all her heart that he had taken less drastic and precipitate measures to remedy his situation.

"No, Benjamin has failed me signally, and is not worth a tallow dip. I'll make no efforts, strenuous or otherwise, to find where he's gone to. I take it you've had no communication from him since his departure from here?" But Cathy was spared telling him a half-truth as he hurried on: "Of course you could not—any billet directed here would come to my notice, and any to Cleveland Row would have been seen by Mrs Wilby: that much I can entrust to her at least," he said blightingly. "So, Catherine—you are all that is left to me now. I trust you don't mean to disappoint me likewise?"

"Oh no, sir! Indeed! I hope not!" she assured him with a fervour which would have surprised her only minutes ago. In truth she had always felt a deep sense of obligation to her guardian, if no great affection, for snatching her from a life of certain penury, and she resolved now to do all that was in her power to recompense him. His wife, she knew, had died after a very few years of marriage; and until today she had thought them childless. That poor boy, incarcerated in a Home

26

all these years! She saw now that it was not wonderful that his lordship should have immersed himself in the establishment of his bank to the exclusion of all else.

"It is a great solace to me to hear your sentiments so properly expressed," he told her. "Indeed you are a credit to me, and I don't regret bestowing the name of Ebford upon you, in any event. Lady Olivia tells me you have taken very well in your first Season. In fact, not a month ago she warned me there would be suitors at my door before long, and as ever she was in the right of it!"

Enlightenment pierced Catherine: so *that* was the purpose of this unprecedented invitation to the Sanctum! The mention of Lady Olivia made her wonder if Christopher had approached his lordship: she could think of no other gentleman who had evinced the least sign of desiring to marry her. Having thought of Chris her perturbation abated a little, and she waited impatiently for him to elaborate.

"I do not scruple to say, young lady, that I had not anticipated a connexion half so desirable! After all, it was not to be thought of, with your lack of family, that you might take the interest of a man of the first consideration," he told her bluntly. "But that, Catherine, is precisely what has come about!"

Could Christopher conceivably be styled 'of the first consideration'? she wondered in a great agitation of spirits. Scarcely, in Society's eyes . . . but perhaps to a banker?

"It gives me immense satisfaction to know that your good schooling, and Lady Olivia's endeavours, have culminated in this very gratifying offer."

Perhaps this sounded a trifle mercenary and calculating even to the ears of a money man, and he hastened to say: "I do not, of course, discount your own charm and amiability, which are far from negligible."

But she was now in far too much of a scare to heed flattery, and she stammered out: "May I know the name of the gentleman, if you please?"

"To be sure you may—that is why you are here!" he responded in quite roguish vein. "Tho' it's true that I may have digressed a little— Honora will be agog by this time, don't you think?" He gave a conspiratorial chuckle, and Catherine thought he seemed to be relishing this colloquy as much as she was hating it. "Mr Lucian Berrington is his name." And even as Catherine's heart lurched within her she could not help but notice the manner in which this was announced; he might have succeeded in snatching the Prince of Orange away from Princess Charlotte for her, from his jubilant reverence. "Such a *very* fortunate girl, you are," he continued similarly. "You have already made his acquaintance, have you not?"

Somehow she found the means to speak. "The— the Mr Berrington who has been here today, sir?"

He positively beamed. "The very fellow!"

"But I——" She was about to protest that she had never set eyes on him to her knowledge, but was cut short by an imperious wave of the hand.

"—Not that you will languish as plain Mrs for over-long, I'm sure of that. Destined for high office, Berrington is. Don't mistake—he is no mushroom. He rose to Lieutenant-Colonel before he sold out, and can boast the very finest family ties. His father was General Sir John Berrington—I suppose you have heard of *that* name. He left him a splendid place in the country, too," he mused a trifle wistfully. He was always on the look-out for a country seat of his own, but was conscious that was in no way the same thing as inheriting a family estate.

She had never heard him speak so volubly or with such animation, and while he continued to sing her unknown lover's praises in like vein she endeavoured to pass in rapid mental review all the male faces she had seen during the course of this very hectic Season. After all, she reasoned, if he was prepared to wed her, must surely have been presented to her at the least! She searched in this mental portrait gallery for a middle-aged to elderly person, military bearing; and, doubtless, unutterably dull, if he cherished political ambitions. There were one or two who might generally be said to have fitted this description, but none had been notable enough to linger in her mind bearing a name. Then she began to question if she were not being naïve to look for even that degree of common knowledge between the parties to an arranged marriage. Far more importantly to the case, Mr Berrington was highly desirable to Ebford's Bank, and therefore to her guardian (Chris had said as much), and she was to be the human bait with which to lure him from Child's; together, no doubt, was a substantial dowry to recompense for her short-comings.

Suddenly she recalled who he was: the top-lofty individual with greying hair whom she had seen dancing attendance upon Lady Olivia more than once. Also he had partnered Melissa for the dance on several occasions, with an air of fine condescension. She herself had stood up with him just once, and of their conversation she could remember not a word. Later she had formed the opinion that he might be Lady Olivia's *cicisbeo*, for her ladyship playfully referred to him as 'The Colonel' and seemed to bask in his attentions. Her husband smiled as broadly upon him as he did on everyone, but Catherine suspected now that the Colonel's high connexions probably lay at the root of his toleration of his wife's admirer. Hitherto she herself had only thought of Mr Berrington as the Colonel, which had caused her present confusion. However, having at last put a face and a figure to his name did nothing to reconcile her to the idea of marrying him; in fact the opposite was true.

So she now found herself placed in a highly unpleasant quandary: only minutes before she had assured her guardian of her devotion to his interests, and now she must upset his plans for her in quite as cruel a fashion as Ben had ever done. In fact, her mutinousness would probably deal him the greater blow of the two, involving as it did the Bank's interests. But she failed to see why she should be expected to sacrifice her entire life for the prospects of a bank! Fast upon that thought came the still less welcome suspicion that it was for some such purpose as this alone that Lord Ebford had housed and educated her: merely as a future pawn in his banking game. The sheer idea of such a devious and long-standing scheme had a powerful effect on her independent nature, and she glared across the desk at its perpetrator.

But Lord Ebford, on home ground once more, was now quite carried away on a happy flood of figures. "—together with investments which yield at least fifteen thousand, Catherine. That's each year," he added patiently. "The precise details of the settlement need not concern you, of course."

Determined to put a stop to this nonsense, she addressed him in a clear, steady voice, and before he could resume his encomium of her unwanted admirer. "I am flattered, of course, that Mr Berrington should pay me the compliment of offering for my hand, but I fear that I cannot accept."

He could not have looked more stunned if he were face to face with a bankrupt client who was refusing to accept a substantial legacy. His dark brows shot up, almost merging for an instant with the sparse hair above. "My dear young lady, it does not lie in your power to accept or reject Mr Berrington as if he were a—a new bonnet! The chief purpose of Lady Olivia's endeavours in presenting you to the town this spring was to secure a husband, as you must know. She has succeeded in that aim, quite surpassing my expectations, and, I'd hazard, her own likewise! She is as yet unaware of your *great good fortune,* of course, as I gave my consent to the match only an hour since."

'Good fortune!' thought Catherine, who was sinking further into black despair with every second. "But am I to have *no* say whatever in my future, sir?" she asked, sounding more plaintive than she intended; for she had already quite resolved that she would never become Mrs Berrington, even if that meant she were casting away the chance to be a duchess one day.

"What is this I hear from you?" he demanded thickly. "You!—who had nothing, and would still

31

have nothing had I not raised you up to stand beside the highest in the land! By God, you forget yourself! And what, pray, is this terrible thing I ask of you?" He flung out his hands in exasperation. "Only that you wed a gentleman possessed of irreproachable worth, a position in life which is near unequalled, and one who could look as high as he pleased for a wife!" Catherine wished fervently that he would.

"In short, as desirable a match as I could have wished for a daughter of my own—and *you* dare to spurn it!" His eyes quite blazed as he said this, and in spite of her own hot feelings she cowered away from him and kept silent.

"And what is it, if I may be permitted to ask, that gives you such a disgust of Mr Berrington?" He was quieter now and trying to curb his wrath, she felt; but had only succeeded in sounding sarcastic.

She could not begin to put her turbulent thoughts into words. "Nothing—nothing at all," she said at last forlornly. "It is only, perhaps, that I had expected my wishes might at least be consulted on this, of all things."

The banker shrugged in total bewilderment. "Mayhap I should have let Lady Olivia divulge it to you—I dare swear you wouldn't have played off these missish airs with her. But I had not the least notion you would be other than overjoyed— how should I?"

For a moment he looked so cast down she felt sorry for him, and, recalling again her earlier promise not to be a disappintment, she felt it must be her duty to agree to the marriage. But then he made it plain once more that her views on the subject were superfluous.

"Well, you will come about in time," he murmured philosophically. His hands were busy again with the papers on the desk, and she sensed that she was about to be dismissed. "I will arrange for the drawing up of the settlement, and in the meantime Berrington wishes you to go down to Challow next week and join his house party there." His fingers closed around the handle of a small silver bell and he rang it. "I'm persuaded I don't need to warn you against any wild notions of the sort your brother had," he went on in minatory tones, and reading her mind with alarming accuracy. "This match is of the utmost importance to me—more important than Benjamin ever was. And if you should try to abscond I would have *you* discovered and fetched home at once, you may depend upon it."

He stood up when Rogers entered, pushing back the heavy chair with a harsh scraping noise. "Take Miss Ebford back to Mrs Wilby." He then turned to the subdued and white-faced Catherine, and smiled as if they were concluding an enjoyable, usual talk. "You may share the splendid news with your aunt, of course, my dear."

THREE

Lady Olivia Dauntry liked to order all as she pleased in life; and on the whole had succeeded in this desire. It might appear from her choice of husband, the eternally merry but hardly prepossessing William, that she had failed in this one respect: but it was not so. Three-and-twenty years before she had selected him from several hopeful suitors. He had then just come into a considerable inheritance, including Melfield, a fine Italianate house in Hertfordshire which particularly appealed to Olivia; and besides that, his boundless optimism and unshakeable affability—tiresome now but more attractive in youth—had always afforded undeniable advantages in ensuring her own way in everything.

She was tall, slim, and elegant of movement. Her face had high cheekbones and fine-modelled features, and was just saved from hardness of expression by a humorous line to the mouth. The china blue eyes were prone to sparkle in the presence of the opposite sex, but with her own kind were more likely to have a measuring look to them. In Society, with her ever-smiling husband, the couple made a blithe impression and could be relied upon to enliven the dullest engagement.

Lord Ebford had early succumbed to those fine eyes and, more recently, had been convinced that her ladyship was the ideal person to launch Catherine into the Polite World on his behalf. But if Lady Olivia had not herself decided earlier that Ebford's Bank needed a partner, and that William was the man, the Banker's scheme would not have prospered.

For it had been plain to her that there would be little direct advantage from chaperoning his ward. Her own daughter, Melissa, had been presented a year before Catherine and, although in her experienced view she was a better prize in the marriage mart than the Ebford girl, for all her prospects she was still unwed and now fast approaching twenty. So Melissa, even if not quite outshone, had a strong rival (made stronger) close at hand. Another contingency, that Christopher, their shy and taciturn son, might fall an easy victim to Catherine's charm and proximity, had also occurred to her. And nothing could be gained from *that* match which had not already been achieved by William acquiring the partnership in Ebford's. Besides, which, she could never quite forget Catherine's questionable origins; the more particularly since her young brother had behaved exactly as one might have expected in such a case.

Lord Ebford had always been most vexingly vague about the circumstances under which he and his late wife had first come upon the foundlings; saying only, in his austere fashion, that they had been happy to accept them into their family and that that must be sufficient recommendation in itself. For once all her powers of cajolery had failed lamentably, and she had never been able to elicit more information on that subject. Not that various possibilities had not risen in her imagination: that the children might be the fruits of a disastrous early marriage which Ebford desired to be expunged from his and everyone else's memory; or that they were natural offspring, accepted by a singularly meek and magnanimous wife. She had never known the latter, an inveterate country dweller and town hater, and so the whole affair remained a still-tantalizing mystery.

That day, she and her daughter were taking a rare and well-earned rest from the exigencies of a very busy Season, in the drawing-room of the Portland Street house. Placed on the northern fringes of London, away from the hurly-burly of Piccadilly and the fashionable squares, Lady Olivia was given to praising the solace of their quiet situation; a claim that was apt to raise the eyebrows of those who had actually visited the residence. For her ladyship had disposed about the drawing-room some quite elegant aviaries of birds—love birds, Java sparrows and parakeets—and, whenever their heads were not under their wings, twitters and shrieks not only obliterated and peace there might be outside, but tended also to engulf all conversation within.

However, their present noise seemed not to

interfere with Melissa's intense study of the latest *Ladies Monthly Museum,* or her mama's deep repose as she lay with her eyes shut on the sofa. Nor did it prevent her ladyship from hearing the click of the door which preceded the entrance of her butler. She was wide awaken when he announced: "Mrs Wilby and Miss Ebford are below, m'lady."

Melissa's eyes brightened, but her mama's did not. What did that pair want? she wondered crossly, and almost had herself denied. But she was not one to shirk her obligations, and besides, it was a trifle unusual for the shrinking Honora to make a call *à l'improviste.* Curiosity overcame fatigue and she bade Sanders to bring them up.

"Melly, come sit by me," she murmured, abandoning her own languid posture and sitting more upright. Casting a sharp eye over her daughter's auburn curls, and the green-and-white striped muslin dress, she leaned forward and twitched the lace neck frills into a more becoming order, to the young lady's annoyance: her mama always contrived never to have a single pleat of her Brunswick cap or Vandyke ruff out of place, she reflected, without loving her for it.

When the visitors were shown in Lady Olivia's eye roved over the apparel of her other young charge. She noted with approval that the chit was wearing her own particular choice of rose silk spencer over a sprigged muslin. But it was not until her gaze lifted to the new Angoulême bonnet that she saw the face beneath it was rather pale and tense.

Their greetings had been mouthed inaudibly against a swell of birdsong; Lady Olivia, as a matter of course, paying scant heed to Honora

Wilby. But now she spared a glance at that lady and observed her countenance was as suffused as Catherine's was pallid.

Perhaps this could have been due merely to Mrs Wilby's attempts to raise her naturally quiet voice above the din, and Olivia rose kindly to shush the nearest birds. It then became apparent that she was being offered a garbled apology of some sort. "—Forgive the intrusion—tried my *utmost* to dissuade dear Cathy—alas, to no avail—insisted. . . ."

Catherine had indeed insisted on calling upon her sponsor as soon as they left the Bank after her fateful *tête-à-tête* with her step-father. She had bundled Mrs Wilby into a hackney, which the porter had summoned for them as usual; but, instead of Bond Street which was their arranged destination (for Hookham's Library) she had bidden the jarvey to convey them to Portland Street.

Mrs Wilby had hardly begun to protest at this when Catherine, in a most excitable manner, poured the whole story of Mr Berrington and her compulsory marriage to him into that astonished lady's ear. When the gist of it was at last more or less clear to her, she remained unable to grasp the central fact that Cathy was not in whoops of joy over such a famous prospect. She supposed for some while that they were merely going to share the glad tidings with Lady Olivia and Melissa. This she considered not quite seemly behaviour, though perhaps understandable in the light of such Wonderful News. When it was borne in upon her that her ladyship's help was to be sought to exert pressure on Lord Ebford—and even Mr Berrington himself!—to retract the offer, she was appalled. Her protestations had continued right up to the moment when the butler opened the drawing-room door for them.

Lady Olivia bestowed one of her coolest stares on Mrs Wilby, then smiled encouragingly at Catherine and held out her hand to her. Melissa, too, was now sensing drama in the air; she lay down her periodical, asking directly: "Cathy, what's wrong?"

Catherine looked wildly from daughter to mother. "I need your aid, ma'am, if you please. You see, I have had—an offer!"

Her ladyship uttered a tinkling laugh which cut through the parakeets with ease. "My dear child! Is that all it is?" She drew the girl down beside her and nodded to Melissa to place a chair for Mrs Wilby. "Now—I trust none of your many admirers has gone beyond the line of what is pleasing? I must say, you do look a trifle *éperdue*." She favoured Mrs Wilby, who sat bolt upright looking increasingly guilt-ridden, with a pungent glance which conveyed that she knew where the blame lay for permitting anything untoward of that nature to occur.

"Oh, no!" exclaimed Catherine. "Nothing of the kind!"

"Well, then, who *is* this gentleman who has upset you? We are all agog to know!" She laughed again, laying a slim hand in a tranquil way on her daughter's arm; although Melissa, for her part, was showing every sign of animated eagerness to hear what had befallen her friend.

Catherine, striving hard for some of her ladyship's admirable dignity, swallowed and said: "Lord Ebford has just informed me that Mr Berrington is desirous of—of marrying me."

"Not the *Colonel?*" Melissa cried, darting a look of astonishment, and apparent outrage, across her mama to Cathy at the far end of the sofa.

This brief comment ended in a subdued yelp of pain, as her mother's fingers dug into her in a way that was part admonition, and partly the consequence of Olivia's having sustained a slight shock. But she addressed Catherine with her former serenity. "Well, I must own that I hadn't at all foreseen an offer from that quarter. Indeed, I cannot think it wholly—suitable. I do wonder why the dear Colonel . . .?" she mused aloud. "But there! I daresay you are over the moon, Catherine!"

"Lord, I should just *think* so!" put in Melissa, only to be restrained by another sharp parental squeeze.

Mrs Wilby sadly shook her head, looking on helplessly while Catherine assured her ladyship in impassioned tones that, far from affording her joy, it was quite the most hateful thing which had ever come her way.

Now perceiving that a crisis loomed which might well call upon all her powers to control, Lady Olivia shifted her grip from Melissa, turned, and clasped both of Catherine's hands comfortingly in her own. "Oh, my dear!—pray calm yourself! You must tell your guardian the strength of your feelings. He is a reasonable man, you know. I am persuaded that he will understand."

"But I *have* told him, and he is *not* a reasonable man! Well, not on this subject, at least," Cathy sniffed. "It is quite true that I *thought* he was— until today. Your la'ship," she went on earnestly, and dropping her voice as much as the avian serenade would allow, "you *must* help me! Will you *please* explain to him yourself that I can't marry Mr Berrington? I don't love him at all, you see. Why, I don't even like him very much!" Then she remembered that he was a friend of Lady Olivia's. "I'm sorry, ma'am, but I don't," she muttered.

Lady Olivia released her hands and then patted them absent-mindedly. "Yes, yes, I do—follow, child."

Honora Wilby broke in at this point in a surprisingly firm voice: "Catherine is overwrought, my lady, as you can see. I believe we should take our leave of you now. Indeed, we should never have intruded here in this ramshcakle style! She will view matters differently when she had had more time to reflect." The chaperon rose stiffly from her chair, but merely drew upon herself another of Lady Olivia's most demolishing looks.

"On the contrary, Mrs Wilby, it was very right that you came: if Catherine feels in need of my counsel and advice at any time, I am sure I am here to give it—and more especially on such a delicate and vital matter as this gives every sign of being to a person of sensibility."

A deep flush of colour appeared on Honora's cheeks as she sank back on to her chair.

"Now, Catherine," her ladyship resumed in a satisfied manner, after this routing of the Wilby Woman, as she always thought of her, "is it perhaps you affect someone else—some *younger* man?"

After a moment's struggle she denied this. Christopher was the only such younger man who came to mind, but she could scarcely reveal that to his mother. "It is simply that I wish to be consulted as to whom I am to wed." she repeated wearily. "Could you not convey that sentiment to Lord Ebford for me?"

"If I thought it would alter the case in any degree, of course I would, silly girl! But it wouldn't serve, you know. Ebford is a man of his word, and if he has told Mr Berrington——"

"Then what *am I to do?*" Catherine demanded shrilly of the room in general. By now, her nerves were at full stretch.

It was her Aunt Wilby who answered, having now made a recover from her set-down. "You will do as you're told, miss, and travel down to Mr Berrington's place in Kent." She spoke with unwonted asperity since Lady Olivia's words to her still rankled, and she felt vaguely that it was all Catherine's fault.

Lady Olivia managed to give the impression of totally ignoring the speaker whilst taking up the point of what she had said. "So, you go to Challow soon?" It was as though she had plucked that intelligence from the air.

"I am invited—which is something quite else. I've no intention of going."

Mrs Wilby clucked with exasperation, and her ladyship found herself for once in reluctant agreement with the Wilby Woman. "Oh, but I think you must," she said slowly. "You have asked for my advice and that is the line of conduct I recommend you follow."

Catherine was shaken to find she could not depend on her support even in this secondary question. "But, ma'am, if I were to——"

"When are you promised to Challow?"

"A sennight hence," said Mrs Wilby as though pronouncing sentence.

"That should be capital," her ladyship said placidly.

"Ma'am, I *cannot* see——"

"No, my dear, I daresay you can't. But these matters call for a certain fineness of touch, you know. It would certainly not do to take this fence in a neck-or-nothing fashion—as the dear Colonel might well put it himself!" She gave a brief trill which drew an answering crescendo from the cages. "I think I may claim to be tolerably well acquainted with the gentleman concerned, and of course with your guardian too. Your instinct to turn to me was very prudent, for if anyone has the power to extricate you from this little imbroglio, I'm sure *I* can do so!"

When the Dauntrys were retiring that night, Lady Olivia dismissed her maid early so that she might have an opportunity to talk to her spouse at some length before he sank into his customary deep and instant slumber.

"William—did Ebford say anything to you about Catherine today?" she called through to him in his dressing-room. She had warned her daughter not to refer to the subject before the family until she herself had broached it with her husband.

"George? No, I don't think so. I believe he had her in to his own room—which was a bit out of the ordinary for him. She didn't stay long: Berrington took up most of his time today." He stuck his grinning pudgy face round the door as he untied his cravat. "I've not the least notion how he has beguiled the fellow, but he's to transfer all his accounts from Child's, I collect."

"Ah, but I know how! He has used Catherine as bait," she said crisply, sitting down before her dressing-table.

His grin broadened still more as he opened the door further to study her expression. "Has he?—the devil! Slim wench and fat dowry, eh? Deuced clever cove, George, you must admit!"

"I'll admit to nothing of the sort."

"But, Livvy, it's a master stroke! George is happy, Berrington's happy, and the Bank's devil-ish happy! Why should you——"

"Catherine is in no wise happy: and I doubt whether Berrington will relish an unwilling bride." She frowned to herself in the glass, wondering why it was not just to her taste to call Berrington 'The Colonel' when speaking of him to William.

"Pooh, the little maid will come about," he opined cheerfully, tossing the disgarded cravat behind him. "She's a taking filly—and, of course, she's blossomed beyond all expectation under your skillful guidance, my love."

"It may not be desirable that Catherine should 'come about'," she retorted, irritated by his husband-like flattery and the total boredom that it overlaid. She leaned forward to the mirror and searched despondingly for wrinkles beneath her eyes. "She is a stubborn girl with a head full of romantical notions, and quite set upon a marriage of attachment or none at all. And I apprehend she is every bit as wilful as that brother of hers."

She looked around as William, now openly bored, was about to disappear into his dressing-room again. "I've had Berrington in my eye for Melissa, you know, any time this six months."

"Well, too late for that now," he said with composure. "For if George has set his mind to this match, then——"

"It is Berrington who signifies in this. It cannot be supposed he truly prefers the Ebford girl to Melly—how could he, why should he? She's a base-born chit. However, franked by Ebford, and rendered a touch of town bronze—*by me, of all people!*—Ebford has been able to gull him into believing he has a good bargain there!" She compressed her lips to invisibility in the looking-glass.

But Mr Dauntry was losing interest once more, and drifting away to continue his disrobing. "I'd let well alone, Liv," he called over his shoulder. "Berrington's downy enough to know what he wants without George telling him! And don't overlook that this way our Bank acquires a valued client—a very valued client indeed."

"And eventually a partner, perhaps?" She let the words hang in the air.

They had the desired effect, for her spouse returned to her a minute later, tying his sombre-hued dressing gown about his bulky figure but now looking distinctly less sleepy. He sat on the padded chest at the foot of the bed, saying: "Why the deuce should he go and make him a partner?"

"Why not? A distinguished son-in-law—and the nearest he will have to family, after all. Berrington's son might well come in the way of inheriting Ebford's, might he not?"

Mr Dauntry laughed outright at this flight of fancy, albeit a shade uneasily. "Blister it, that's looking ahead!"

"No more than Ebford is, I'll warrant," she said dryly.

"But what of Christopher? Now, he really might rise to be partner. You have forgotten him in these—ah—projections, my love?"

"No, I have not. For how will he ever acquire a partnership, do you suppose? On your example, perhaps?—or on your money? He still has little enough of his own beyond that independence from my mother."

Mr Dauntry, whose ear was quick for her inflexions of tone on those occasions when he was actually listening to her, caught the unkind emphasis laid on the word 'example'; and wondered how much Olivia knew of his banking affairs.

He knew she was as thick as inkle weavers with George over the girl; but surely George wasn't one to discuss their recent little disagreements over that generous credit he had offered to certain clients? No, of course not: Ebford was notoriously stiff-rumped about such paltry things, or else he wouldn't have cut up so rusty over the wretched loans in the first place. He was emphatically not the man to divulge banking business to his partner's wife. He relaxed, saying: "I'll grant Chris this much—he's a banker through and through. He'll make into a damned good partner some day." He paused, before reluctantly broadening the subject from business partnerships to the matrimonial variety. "Y'know, I had thought he and the Ebford girl might—y'know. But with Berrington in the field—well, the boy ain't quite Golden Ball, as you just said: and that's who he'd need to be to get his nose in front of Berrington!" This racing allusion made him laugh, and he was promptly seized with a violent fit of coughing which brought some colour even to his parchment face.

Lady Olivia sighed, and resumed scrutiny of her own complexion until the paroxysm subsided. Then, before he could launch into another irrelevant comment, she said to him: "Let me make one thing very clear: I *do not* wish Christopher to wed that chit of Ebford's. What would we glean from such a *great sacrifice* that we don't have already from your partnership? In any event, I know Ebford has more sense than you, and cherishes the very highest aspirations for her—as, indeed, he is proving only too clearly at this present."

He was inured to such frankness from her and seemed quite unoffended. "Mm. Y'know, Livvy, it puzzles me not a little that you didn't have time to catch what was in the wind between Berrington and the girl before now."

She looked at him sharply; were it anyone else, she would have suspicioned that he was voicing a criticism of her chaperonage, or even, perhaps, of her close association with the Colonel. But surely not! No, not William!

Any small doubt still lingering in her mind vanished as a far more pressing thought pushed it out. "Wait! I wonder if Berrington has been led on to think that Catherine is Ebford's *own* daughter?"

He eyed her with secret amusement, saying lazily: "George wouldn't have the gall."

"Wouldn't he, though? Remember, very few people are privy to the facts of the case. Why, the whole has not been made known even to me—but I know enough," she concluded ominously.

Mr Dauntry's tolerant amusement was now dispelled, and he addressed her in stern accents. "Now look, Olivia—you aren't to go tittle-tattling to Berrington! A fine dust you'll kick up if you do—and all to damnable purpose! Let the matter rest! for pity's sake don't give Berrington a disgust of Ebford: the Bank stands much in need of his connexions, and his fortune, just now."

"Oh, make yourself easy," she told him airily. "If Berrington can be *persuaded* a little to think of Melissa—and it is a match that becomes increasingly desirable to me the more I consider it—then very soon you won't care a fiddlestick for Ebford or the partnership, have you thought of that? You would be in a fair way to setting up your own bank, with Berrington franking you!"

He stared back at her, losing himself again in private reflection. The prospect she had just held out to him, while being highly speculative and not a little preposterous, did not altogether fail to interest him after that last uncomfortable parley he had endured with George Ebford. Although he knew his wife well enough, he was not generally as astute as he fancied himself. Even so, he was well able to perceive other shoals in the future with George over their differing policies at the Bank. But that he would be ill-suited to running his own establishment did not occur to him, for such self-knowledge had always been swamped by the easy flow of his confidence as he proceeded through life.

While he was thus deliberating, Lady Olivia was continuing to expound her plan.

"It is crucial that Melly should accompany Catherine to Challow, but I think I shall not go with them. The Season is by no means ending yet, but will be prolonged until after Wellington returns in triumph from the Continent—I had that from Lady Jersey only last week." She removed the stopper from the Gowlands Lotion and began applying some to her perfectly smooth forehead. "But such matters are of no interest to the young . . . Melly will be very ready to leave town and set about captivating Berrington—and more particularly when it is pointed out to her that she will be rendering her dear friend the greatest service. Our Poppet may have her faults, but I will say for her that she's not one to allow her heart to rule her head. As for poor Catherine, she will present no obstacle to the scheme because of her stupid attitude, and little will be asked of her: it will suffice if Berrington merely wounds himself on the thorns of her mislike of him. Not but what she must be told what is afoot, else she could inadvertently blight Melly's chances. Yes, that Wilby Woman—*for once*—is the ideal chaperon for this visit, and will not know where to *begin* to order her charges!" she concluded, clapping her hands together in delight. Her mouth took on a complacent curve and her eyes danced. "Now, William— tell me this is not the most splendid design you ever heard, and simply bound to succeed?"

But William, for whom those fine eyes had sparkled rarely of late, missed them on this occasion also; he was fast asleep, grizzled head slumped forward on his chest, and emitting a faint snore which sounded a sardonic commentary on what she had been at such pains to tell him.

FOUR

Once Lady Olivia had referred to the dire prospect of her marriage as 'this little imbroglio', Catherine abandoned hope of any real assistance coming from that quarter. Even in the hackney going home to Cleveland Row in St James's, she had already made up her mind that her only chance of salvation lay in Christopher.

Consoling herself that there was still a week in which to rummage up a scheme of sorts, she faced her guardian at dinner with a certain stoicism. He for his part fully expected she must realize her good fortune sooner or later, and did not advert to the subject again on his return home.

It had long been fixed that she should join the Dauntry party the following day for a visit to the theatre, and she hoped the opportunity would arise sometime during the evening for a private word with Chris. However she could not be sanguine about this because, although her aunt was not to accompany them on this occasion, Lady Olivia rarely relaxed her vigilance upon the two of them. So when she followed their groom, who was carrying the bandbox containing her evening clothes, up to the entrance of the Dauntry residence, she lacked her usual sense of happy anticipation when going there.

Once in the familiar hall she acknowledged Sanders' welcoming words in an abstracted fashion, for she was now in hourly dread of coming smash up against Mr Berrington, who was often to be found in the company here; and she was suddenly quite certain he would be here now. No doubt it had been planned that he should be. . . .

She was half-aware that she was not being quite reasonable on the subject of her suitor; but could not help herself. When he had held no significance or even interest for her, she had been well able to withstand his quelling stares. (For her urgent need to remember at least something more about him had by now called to her mind an assembly not long ago, when a tall and austere figure had put up his glass at her most steadily as she went down the dance.) Now, though, she did not know how she would go on if that same figure was soon bearing down upon her, full of hideous import.

But for the moment, and to her intense relief, the only person who came to meet her was Melissa, and she seemed exceptionally effusive. Only when she drew her in the direction of the morning-parlour did Catherine stiffen again.

"Melly—*who is in there?*"

"Only mama, peagoose! Whom did you suppose?" Melissa's fine eyes, of a jade-like hue, widened in sudden comprehension. "Lord, are you *so* afraid of the Colonel?"

"Not afraid, precisely, no. But you must see I am placed in an intolerable situation! Would you not feel my sentiments if you had just been told, out of the blue, that you were to be the wife of a complete stranger?"

Melissa shrugged. "That might depend upon the stranger."

She surveyed her in amazement. "But if it were . . . Mr Berrington?"

"He is well enough—and undeniably a notable *parti*," Melissa returned, with a drawling detachment that would have seemed wonderful to anyone who had listened to her on the subject of the Colonel upon previous occasions. "Come *on,* Cathy, mama has something she wishes to say to you on this very matter."

The two girls were much of a height, and Melissa now placed her arm firmly about Catherine's slender waist and fetched her at last into the morning-parlour.

She found the next few minutes positively stunning, and her heart began to beat like a great clock inside her breast as her ladyship's imperturbable tones continued. She had a way of presenting things that, for a time at least, masked her incredible proposal that her daughter had *carte blanche* and her full blessing to seduce the Colonel. Catherine was aghast, and could only look, with her face aflame, at her friend and then back at Lady Olivia.

But finally she burst forth: "Oh, *no ma'am!* I

would not hear of it! I could not allow poor Melissa to sacrifice herself so for my sake! And besides—it might not answer," she added in a smaller voice, realizing this accorded ill with the high morality of her initial response.

Lady Olivia fixed her with a look that was totally at variance with the smile upon her lips. "Catherine," she said straitly, "do you or do you not wish to be free of your obligation to wed the Colonel?"

She bit her lip and nodded wretchedly. "Of course I do—but not in this way."

"Which way would you choose, then? I do not recall that you were overflowing with schemes yesterday to terminate the match—unless your head is still so hot that you would have me go to Berrington and tell him you hold him in mislike!" Her ladyship laughed unpleasantly. "I can think of nothing so likely to set a man on his mettle, and render you a more desirable prize to him than ever."

Catherine said slowly: "Melly—would you *willingly* bear a part in all this?"

"For you, yes," was the demure reply.

"But what of your reputation?—cast to the winds, and just for me!"

"You have not understood completely, I fear," resumed her ladyship. "Melissa's purpose in 'all this' is to usurp your position in its entirety, and wed the Colonel in your place."

This calm pronouncement induced some moments of total silence; then Catherine whispered to her friend: "But why ever should you? Only minutes ago you said Mr Berrington——"

"She will do so because she has the good sense to

see that the Colonel is a matrimonial prize of the first rank. And if you will only *think*, Catherine, you will come to realize that Melissa is admirably placed to step into your shoes in all circumstances: Berrington will still be enabled to have his precious connexion with the Bank through my husband, and so Ebford will not take exception on that head. By the by—you will not, of course, breathe a word of this conversation to your guardian, or, indeed, to anyone else."

Catherine swallowed, looking down at her feet. Now that the shock of these revelations was slightly lessening, she could begin to perceive a certain shameless cogency behind them. Even so, she felt vaguely that Lady Olivia might not be right in regard to Lord Ebford's complaisance at such extraordinary developments, and she opened her mouth to say that; but her ladyship was now in full rhetorical flood and brooking no interruptions.

"I have not as yet ascertained whether the dear—whether the Colonel is still fixed in town or has already left for Challow. He has not cared overmuch for all the junketing to do with these Victory celebrations—soldiers don't like that kind of thing, you know—and so I own it wouldn't surprise me if he has already returned into Kent."

"Oh, good!" Catherine exclaimed involuntarily, drawing down upon her a further look of crushing admonition.

"However, there will be no difficulty in securing his agreement to Melissa's travelling down with you. I have already written to Ebford, saying all that he would expect me to at your good fortune—and mentioned to him that Melissa would be going down to Challow with you. My note to the

Colonel I had carried by messenger to Duke Street—but that would reach him at Challow well before next week." Her ladyship's mouth now became a little wry. "Of course I tendered him my congratulations, and told him that you have a particular desire for Melissa to be at your side for the house party." She frowned, aware of some detail in these various ruthless dispositions which was not yet smoothed out to her satisfaction. "It would be of immense assistance if he were still in town, for then I might commence the business of instating Melissa in your place without delay," she concluded vexedly, and with total lack of abashment. However, even she thought it best to forbear from adding that her prime weapon in this campaign was to denigrate Catherine in the dear Colonel's eyes by ensuring that he knew the whole as to the girl's doubtful origins; and even she had felt that could not be conveyed by letter quite tastefully.

Catherine merely marvelled at this flow of confidence, and hoped with all her heart that it was not misplaced.

"We will equal whatever undertakings Ebford has made in your settlement, of course. As this is so clearly a *mariage de convenance,* I cannot foresee any great difficulty." She finally broke off to examine the two agitated damsels in front of her, frankly measuring the attractions of one against the other.

Uncomfortably aware of the partial nature of this scrutiny, and still reeling from this formidable presentation of the case, Catherine found herself supposing that there was no reason (sensibility aside) why Melissa should not take her place as

Berrington's bride. Certainly she cherished no illusions as to her friend's superiority in appearance: those crisp auburn curls were of a different order from her own lanky waving dark locks, forever needing curl papers; and her own blue-grey eyes went simply unseen near Melissa's beautiful greenish orbs. And added to the better looks was her infinitely superior birth; in fact, the sole equality between them was that they had both received their education at the same establishment —though even here Melissa's extra year had added a polish which Catherine knew she lacked. Surely, then, the Colonel must prefer her, if the terms were the same, rather than be obliged to share his future with a dowdy, contumacious, very unwilling wife in the shape of herself? Indeed, she was almost convinced that this must be so by the time Lady Olivia left them to dress for the theatre.

"Don't delay your own dressing too long with gossip, my dears," she bade them cheerfully before closing the door.

When they were alone, the pair exchanged speculative silent glances; Melissa's face full of impudence and excitement, Catherine's still burdened with shock and apprehension.

"Oh, come on, pluck up," the former said presently. "It will be famous fun—you'll see!"

"Both you and your mama speak of it as if it were a game. . . ."

Melissa wrinkled her *retroussé* little nose. "Well, Cathy, it *is*, in a way. The whole season, I mean, and this business of finding a husband! And I must own I would as lief marry the Colonel as any other of my set of *pretendents*. They are mostly such greenhorns—and no one could level that word at Mr Berrington!"

"I take it that you are . . . well acquainted with him?" Catherine murmured striving to maintain the worldly tone of this conversation.

"Well, you must have observed that mama and he are monstrously close. Indeed, at one time I thought they must be lovers—but I think not, you know," she said blandly, and putting her listener's new-found worldliness in some peril. "Tho' it's true he lived in our pockets for some while after his return from the Peninsula."

"When was that?" Catherine interposed quickly, glad to ask an innocuous question and add to her knowledge of the evidently odious Colonel.

"Not much above a year ago, to the best of my recollection. Yes, it must have been, for I quit that horrid seminary about the same time." She hesitated a second, sophistication vying with curiosity, then said in a rush: "It amazes me vastly that *you* are not better acquainted with Berrington. After all, you spent a good deal of that summer with us at Melfield, didn't you?"

"There were always so many guests, and I fear I paid little regard to your parents' friends," she said vaguely, not really listening.

"Yes, I see. . . ." Although in fact Melissa was quite at a loss to fathom how one of her sex could disregard a presentable gentleman of any age. "Well," she went on briskly, "it is my private belief that mama was a trifle miffed when she learned that the Colonel had offered for you—and behind her back, so to speak. She always nourished hopes in that quarter for me, you see, which explains in some sort her own attachment to him.

So, Cathy, you need not feel that what I am proposing to do is *so* untoward," she declared.

It was Catherine's turn to be at a loss. "No, perhaps not," she said slowly. She had noticed that Melissa's gaze kept wandering away towards the door, and that was beginning to make her uneasy; more fancies of Berrington's hidden presence rushed upon her. She said in a loud voice: "Should we not go and change?"

"No, not yet." Melissa gave her a conspiratorial smile which reassured her not at all. "Chris is supposed to be joining us. I told him he must—but he is so vastly shy there is no doing anything with him, the nodcock!"

Despite this sisterly encomium Catherine felt a surge of relief that he was coming; but they would have to be alone if she were to appeal to him for help. "Does he know about—everything?"

"Lord, yes, I told him right away. Well, I had to! You must know he has a *tendre* for you: but it requires a spur of his nature to bring one such as *him* to a declaration!"

Catherine had scarcely recovered her countenance over this final piece of managing from a member of the Dauntry family, when Christopher at last put in a typically hesitant appearance.

"Oh—ah!—I'm sorry! Miss Ebford, your very obedient . . . don't wish to intrude. . . ."

"Come, in, Chris, and stop talking fustian. We are all well aware of why we're here," said Melissa roundly, and causing her brother's healthy complexion to attain an even ruddier hue.

If he had difficulty meeting her eye on the more usual occasions when they met, it seemed doubly hard for him now. Speech, too, eluded him until he

59

mumbled: "Dash it, no call to put Miss Ebford to the blush, Melly."

"No, there is no need whatever," Melissa said tartly, rising to her feet. "For I am going up to dress: pray don't be too long after me, Cathy!" And, with a saucy wink at her friend, she almost skipped from the room.

Handed this golden opportunity, Catherine could think of nothing, at first, to say to him beyond a helpless: "Won't you sit down, Christopher?"

He declined, and took instead to restless pacing. "Little did I dream," she then launched off breathlessly, "when I asked you about Mr Berrington yesterday, what his *purpose was* in being there!"

"No!—No, indeed!" His tone was a little strangulated but he seemed on the whole relieved that she had introduced the subject directly. "Melly gave me the lie of it as soon as I got home: couldn't credit it. Oh!—crave your pardon! Didn't mean quite that! The thing is, you're an out-and-outer: bound to have offers—dozens of 'em!"

She smiled ruefully, "I haven't, you know. This is the first, and I wish it—together with Mr Berrington—at the ends of the earth!"

"Then you're determined not to accept?"

"Yes, utterly! Do you recall you said Mr Berrington was worth a banker bartering his soul away for? Well—*I* shall not figure as a convenient pawn in my guardian's banking game."

He checked his perambulations about the room and looked at her with one of the solemn stares which added several years to his age. "I see. No one can deny Berrington is a slap-up fellow," he mused gravely. "I mean, a career like his in Spain. . . . He must have caught the Duke's own eye, you know: how else to soar to Lieutenant-Colonel in no more than a flea's leap? And one of the warmest men in town—small wonder old Ebford's cock-a-hoop. A dashed hard cove to send to the rightabout," he concluded with a shake of his head.

Catherine was a little unnerved, not having bargained for a eulogy upon the Colonel at this juncture. "Christopher—I do *not* require a good commander, or a financial genius, but, one day perhaps, a kind and loving husband. I should not care if he was much, much poorer than the Colonel. Can't you understand?—*I am being sold to the highest bidder!*"

"Dash it, that's doing it too brown, as you well know."

"No, it isn't! And it's an antique, barbarous notion, as anyone must see—as *you* must see above most others, or so I would have——" She groped for her handkerchief, adding wearily: "Look, we may not have much time. . . ." She glanced at the door, fearful lest her raised voice had been heard outside. "And I must have some help. Melissa has told you we go down to Challow only next week, I collect?"

"Yes, yes, she did." His sister had also made known to him—in distressingly plain terms—that if he did not desire to forfeit all respect as a gentleman, he would forthwith snatch Catherine from the Colonel's mercenary clutch by leading her himself to the altar—at Gretna Green should that prove inevitable. Whilst he was still reeling from that stern judgement, she had delivered him another weighty blow by announcing that she

61

herself was prepared to Sacrifice All for her dearest friend by taking her place as the Colonel's bride.

Christopher, who did not want for sense precisely, but who had not been blessed with a great depth of understanding of the female mind, had been left in a state of inner turmoil by Melissa's confidences. Indeed, it had taken every ounce of his resolution, and his real regard for Catherine, to step into the morning-parlour and set eyes upon the one who harboured such great expectancies of him.

"She is a true friend," said Catherine with fervour, still speaking of Melissa, "and has agreed to a—a *ruse* to extricate me from my plight. But I own I cannot like it—and that aside, I don't believe it will serve the trick." She hesitated, not wishing to be the one to enlighten him beyond his knowledge. "So, I would still prefer to hold to my original scheme of not going to Challow at all."

"Not go? But surely you must?" He was looking down at her in seeming astonishment; and quite forgetting the heroic role reserved for him by his sister.

"No—as I have not the smallest intention of marrying him, then I cannot accept his hospitality."

"Well, if you are quite resolved upon——"

"I am." She let the ensuing pause drag out a little, until it became clear that Christopher was not about to suggest that he rode off with her on his saddle bow. It occurred to her then that perhaps his inherent bashfulness was her other great misfortune in the present crisis: she could not imagine even a conventional proposal ever springing readily to his lips. At last she sighed, gave up, and interjected: "You see, I just need somewhere

where I might hide for a while until all the brouhaha dies down—I thought, perhaps, a cottage on your family estate?"

His jaw dropped. "You mean at Melfield?"

"Yes. I'm persuaded Lady Olivia wouldn't cast a serious rub in the way if she knew it, as she is conniving at Melissa's plan to help me." Which—though blunt enough—was putting it mildly, she thought. "Your sister could still travel to Kent, of course, and, er, distract the Colonel." This made Melissa sound like some sort of concubine, and Catherine instantly regretted the remark; but her thoughtful auditor seemed not to hear it.

"I'd do any dashed thing to help, of course," he declared at last. "Yes, by Jove, if that's what you want! Happy to oblige!" His smile was still a little tentative, but she felt nevertheless that he was warming to the idea now that he had fully apprehended how much she was in earnest.

Sensing that no more could be expected from him at the moment, she stood up and smiled back at him with gratitude. "Chris, you have taken a great burden from my shoulders. To have just one person I can depend on is all I ask." She stretched out her hand in impulsive fashion, then reddened a little.

"Yes, well," he murmured, but taking it in his own spontaneously. "You *can* depend upon me; I'll come up with some shift or other to meet the case."

"Thank you. I really cannot convey how grateful I am." Although her faltering tones confirmed the veracity of the sentiment very fully, and he squeezed her hand in response. She felt at peace for the first time since receiving the Hideous

Offer. "It will soon be time for us to leave for the theatre," she managed to say at last, regaining command of her voice and her hand.

"Lord, yes, I'd quite forgot—Kean in The Moor, ain't it?"

"Yes: do you know if he plays Othello or Iago this time?"

"I've not the least notion! Nor do I promise, in the circumstances, to be able to tell you at curtain drop, either!"

She felt stricken with guilt. "Poor Chris—I'm truly sorry to have mazed you in this fashion."

Suddenly he grinned. "Devil a bit! I'll contrive for you to give friend Berrington the bag, never fear!"

FIVE

But the day for Catherine's departure for Challow continued to approach inexorably; and, to her dismay, all that Christopher had 'contrived' thus far was a ride in the Park.

He had invited her to accompany his sister, together with Mr Gerrard Coleby, one of Melissa's much-maligned younger admirers, and himself, three days after receiving her plea for help.

Mr Coleby, a regular Dash whose spectacular brass coat buttons proclaimed him to be at least an aspirant to high fashion, had needed little encouragement from Melissa to canter ahead with her when the party neared the Apsley Gate, leaving Catherine and Christopher together.

"Well, what news?" she asked him at once. Until that moment she had told herself that his serious and taciturn mien was his customary one, and signified nothing: now, when his face took on a still more dejected aspect, all buoyancy left her and she sank hopelessly into the stiff side-saddle.

"I will not pretend to you. . . . I have achieved nothing as yet. Don't look like that!—it really is my most earnest desire to help you. But the devilish thing is, I can see no conformable way."

She could not suppress an impatient little laugh. "No, I'm persuaded there are no *conformable* ways, Christopher! What of Melfield?"

He broke off his rapt study of his mount's ears and glanced across at her. "As to that, I fear mama would not be as compliant as you suppose. She seems quite set upon your going to Challow—I cannot think she would aid and abet us were you to, er, disappear just now."

In fact, from one or two indications he had received in the past from his parent, he was tolerably sure she did not favour his taking a particular interest in Catherine, even when her affairs weren't as havey-cavey as in the present case. Being good-natured, and very fond of all the members of his family as well as of Catherine, he knew he was not made of the stuff which defied maternal wishes with ease in order to marry, and the fact he had now attained his majority altered that conflict of feeling very little. He gave a heavy sigh; his prospects with his fair companion now seemed more arid than ever, for he was well aware that Lord Ebford was perhaps even less ready than his mother to welcome him in Berrington's stead. He also perceived that his own future at the Bank was most awkwardly entangled with the whole wretched business.

"Haven't you some friend *you* could turn to for

help?" she asked, as the silence between them stretched out.

"Of course I've thought of that, but consider, it would need to be someone ready to face the combined wrath of two very powerful men when the scheme was exposed—which it certainly would be, in the end," he said gloomily.

"Not if I am lost in some northern fastness."

He snorted. "Catherine, pray understand we are not concocting a tale for the Minerva Press! What gammon do we tell your benefactors in this *fastness* when you reach there? In any case I could not countenance your going about the country unattended."

"Or perhaps Ireland would offer a refuge," she went on, ignoring this irresolute talk.

He took a deep, patient breath. "I don't know a soul in Ireland, do you?"

"No," she agreed bleakly, kicking her cold feet to life against the footstall. A chilling wind was now moving the leaves on the big trees and raising dust on the surface of the Drive. Christopher plucked sharply with his riding hand and they moved forward at a quickened gait.

The motion seemed to restore his temper and good sense. "Now look here," he said reasonably. "Have you means at your disposal to support yourself for any time?"

"No," she said again, further dispirited. She did not want to imperil his better frame of mind by suggesting that she could go for a governess, or a companion, knowing he would disapprove strongly. Indeed, such desperate shifts daunted her more than a little, though she knew she would turn to them if all else failed.

"Then, I beg you, give up this caprice! *I know* it can only cause mischief."

Again she wisely held her tongue and they rode on in silence for several minutes until she said coolly: "I collect you believe I should submit to these—these nuptials, however detestable I find them?"

"Well, dash it, no, not if you put the thing like that! But really that ain't the way of it at all. Berrington's no medieval monster who'd take an unwilling bride. If your guardian's too bedazzled at the chance of laying his hands on all his rolls of soft to take no for an answer, then what you should do is go to Challow and tell the man to his face that you won't have him!"

For the first time Christopher now sounded masterfully sure of himself, and though she appreciated that, it also made her fire up. "You sound just like your mama—and you both make it sound so easy to do the various things you suggest! But you cannot understand, being a man, and of age. I think Lord Ebford would turn me out without a penny if I fail him—especially after Ben's behaviour. Frankly, I would liefer run away now than wait for that to happen. For what have I to lose—except a most disagreeable encounter with Mr Berrington?"

Christopher looked increasingly alarmed. He reined in his horse and leaned across to check her own animal, saying urgently: "Please—for my sake—abandon this idea of absconding! Only think what a coil it would make!—I should be out of my wits with worry for you!"

She had never heard such an impassioned speech from him, and the obvious sincerity of it touched her deeply. Through no fault of his own he had been placed in a most unhappy position. Looking at him now, it was borne in upon her that he might well be on the brink of making her a reluctant proposal, merely to prevent her flight. And if he ever *did* propose to her, she wanted reluctance to play no part in it. . . . "Very well," she said levelly, "but what am I to do after I have rejected Mr Berrington?"

"Good girl!" Relief flooded his face and he broke into a rare broad smile. "There's no need to do anything daffish at all: we'll try a fresh cast once you're back from Kent, and, if Ebford does turn you out, I'm sure you'll be welcome to stay at Portland Street for as long as you wish. After all, you will have done what mama wants by then."

This prompted her to ask: "You do know why Melissa is to accompany me?"

"Oh yes: I hear she is to throw out lures and bring the Colonel to his knees!" he said in withering tones. "All I can say is, if he prefers her to you he must be a Bedlamite—which he very definitely ain't! Why, you can see that that Joyous Spirit in front of us now with Melly is *her* notion of an eligible! *My sister,* contriving to ensnare one such as the Colonel?——Ha!"

She was startled to hear such blighting sentiments from the lenient Chris, until she remembered that Melissa expressed herself very similarly where he was concerned. No doubt it was just an example of brother-and-sister bickering; though if he were right in his opinion, it did not bode well for the success of Melissa's stratagem on her behalf. Depression began to eat into her again.

He cast her an uncomfortable glance as they

once more trotted forward. "Suppose I shouldn't have said that—but, dash it, it's true enough! If you ask me, mama's an addlepate to think Melly can bring the thing off."

"Well, *I* think there is every reason to suppose that this Mr Berrington will succumb to your sister's very considerable attractions," she said roundly, and with a mixture of loyalty and defiance. "I shall certainly do all I can to throw them in each other's path, if I go." She caught his stern eye and added submissively: "Very well—*when* I go."

At that point in the conversation Melissa was seen to be galloping back to them, with her colourful admirer in hot pursuit. "God, what a fellow!" Christopher said with intensity. "Right—that's finally agreed, then. You're not to run off anywhere, or do any other hoydenish cut-ups, until you've met the ogre face to face, eh? Tell Melly to be sure to let me know the day of your return."

"Oh—but will you not find some way of escorting us back to town yourself?" Although she had scarcely been able to concentrate on such details as yet, she was alarmed at this bland talk of her 'return'—as if all she had to do was summon a hackney in the depths of Kent.

He appeared slightly taken aback, but said: "Yes, to be sure—easiest thing in the world."

Catherine just had time to thank him before the other pair came thundering up to them in a cloud of dust; whereupon the two Dauntrys exchanged several remarks in much the same critical style that they were wont to employ in each other's absence.

Two days later Catherine accompanied some members of that family to a dress-party, which had been arranged before The Offer was made. Christopher had cried off from the engagement, preferring to be out on the town with his cronies, according to Lady Olivia: but this was not his usual form of amusement, and Catherine thought it more likely that his mother was keeping them apart. However, her ladyship also vouchsafed the intelligence that Mr Berrington was now definitely gone into the country, so she was able to face the evening without fear of an encounter with him.

It proved to be the dullest of gatherings enlivened for her only by the latest *on dit* concerning Princess Charlotte. Rumours were gathering credence that her marriage to the Prince of Orange was to be called off. The Princess of Wales, it was said, had not approved the match and had somehow over-ridden the Regent's wishes. When she heard of this, Catherine suddenly wished that she had a mother who would protect her interests so fiercely. It was now being borne in upon her that men made unreliable matchmakers. She wondered if the Royal predicament accounted for the Princess's mulish looks the day she had seen her: somehow, this latest event made her feel closer to her exalted 'twin' than ever before.

They were to travel to Challow on the last Saturday in June. The whole of Friday was occupied with packing, over which there was a good deal of friction between Catherine and her aunt.

Lord Ebford had never engaged a lady's maid for Catherine; regarding that expenditure as unnecessary; for whenever she went into Society it was via Portland Street, and after availing herself of the services of Lady Olivia's dresser, Miss Acton.

A very capacious trunk had been sent over to Cleveland Row the day before by her ladyship. This was from the Dauntry travelling chaise which was to carry Melissa, Catherine, Miss Wilby and Miss Acton to Challow. Under this arrangement Lord Ebford had not been called upon to sacrifice his own carriage for the day; which had largely reconciled him to the fact that Melissa was to go with Catherine. The Banker was not overfond of Lady Olivia's daughter, discerning in her character certain attributes of which he could not approve, but he could hardly object to her going to Challow if, as he had been led to understand, Berrington had invited her. The Dauntrys being old friends of the Colonel, he had no cause to look upon the invitation as anything untoward.

Catherine eyed the vast box without enthusiasm. "But I shall not need anywhere near so much space for a stay of only a few days!" She had spared her aunt the knowledge that even this was an exaggeration, and that the bald fact was she intended to inform their host at the outset she would not be his; and then depart as soon as may be.

However she forbore from further comment until Mrs Wilby picked up her riding habit. "No, I certainly don't want that," she said in trenchant tones: a lack of suitable garb would enable her to refuse any suggestion that she should accompany her host out riding. Or was it the fact that she had chosen the cloth for that dress because it was the exact shade of Christopher's *bleu celeste* coat, that made her wish to leave it behind on this occasion?

72

Her aunt merely looked perplexed and said: "Of course you will!—you are going into the country." Then, clucking under her breath, she added it to the growing pile of clothes in the trunk.

Catherine sighed, and endeavoured to refrain from more criticism as her aunt bustled about the bedroom in a sea of gowns, *chemises-de-nuit*, and silver paper. But when the very best ball dress, of French gauze and pink silk, was lovingly removed from its permanent home she felt compelled to voice a final protest. "Now, even you cannot say *that* is *de rigeur* for a country house party!"

Honora's plump features assumed an expression that was at once both troubled and stubborn. "You think not, dear? But surely there is bound to be a dress-party, at the very least, for the announcement of the betrothal? Oh dear—this is something her ladyship would know," she murmured unhappily.

"An *announcement*—so soon?" Catherine's voice was quite shrill, for she had really not thought of such a thing; so anxious had she been to disentangle herself before such formalities could conceivably occur.

"Well, yes, I think . . . that is, I am persuaded Ebford said something of the sort. At least, I thought he did so. . . . Oh, *I* don't know!"

Catherine now perceived that her aunt was fast being reduced to a quaking jelly by all these uncertainties and aggravations, and felt a stab of guilt: she knew her own behaviour must be eroding what little confidence Honora possessed. "Then it will be safer if we take it, will it not?" she said gently. The older woman quite beamed with relief, and began the delicate task of folding the silk and gauze confection away into the trunk.

As they were to travel on a Saturday, at one point it had been in Catherine's agitated mind to be laid low at the last moment by a sudden totally incapacitating head- or tooth-ache. That would have gained her a reprieve at least until Monday, as they never journeyed on the Sabbath. However, apart from the difficulty of deceiving her aunt, who was oddly astute on all matters concerning ill-health, she had decided that she would as lief go down to Challow without further prevarication. No useful purpose could be served by delaying her momentous meeting with Mr Berrington: the sooner it was behind her, then the sooner she would return to town and throw herself on Lady Olivia's mercy. She realized full well that there would be no point in her coming back to Cleveland Row. Lord Ebford's reception of her in such circumstances was not in the slightest doubt; and she could well imagine him escorting her grimly all the way back to Kent.

In spite of his attitude it still grieved her to be forced to destroy his hopes in this way. She had not forgotten the unspeakable tragedy of his imbecile son, locked away somewhere; while of course the memory of Ben's abscondence was with her constantly.

Brushing tears away from Mrs Wilby's sight, she wished her wilful young brother had paused just a while longer before taking flight. For *he* would have known how to help her. They could have run away together, then, and started a new life.

SIX

No Divine Intervention, or more mundane difficulty, occurred to prevent the prompt arrival of
the Dauntry travelling chaise in Cleveland Row
at nine o'clock on Saturday morning.

Mrs Wilby, who had risen at six, and Catherine,
who had been awake long before that hour, had
only to draw on their gloves and take their leave
of Lord Ebford before following the now fully-
laden trunk down to the waiting equipage.

His lordship stepped from the study in his calm
and deliberate way as soon as the chaise wheels
were heard grinding the gravel outside. He had
breakfasted with the departing ladies, but conversation was always minimal on that occasion;
he had an arrangement for a special early deliv-
ery of post to the house, and today, as usual, had
made a point of reading his letters at the table
before setting off for the Bank.

"Well, now," he said finally to Catherine, "the great day has come at last, eh?" His face relaxed from its habitual cast and he smiled at her in a way which, she knew, was truly benevolent. Her lip quivered as he took her hand in his firm grip.

He had not realized, because of his letter-reading, that she had eaten scarcely a morsel of breakfast, and now the gloves effectively concealed her icy fingers from his notice. But he did observe her general appearance, and frowned. "What's this? No fine feathers for the occasion? I suppose you know best, but drab brown don't seem the thing to me—what of that pretty pink affair I've seen you in sometimes?"

Whereupon he turned his penetrating gaze on to Honora, who was quite resigned to bearing the blame for any shortcomings in her ward, whether real or imaginary, and so was not especially discomposed by this present censure. But as Aunt Wilby had herself recommended the pink, Catherine felt bound to defend her. "I think this is the more practical choice for travelling, sir, being of a dark hue." She had in fact chosen it in accord with her absolute resolve to appear as unalluring as was humanly possible throughout the short duration of her country visit.

He grunted. "Well, if you say so—only I don't wish for Berrington to deem me a pinchfist."

She was able just then to draw his attention to the laden trunk, which was causing some exertion to his porter and the Dauntry groom as they struggled with it to the door.

"Ah! Good! Capital!" Basically he was in sanguine mood today and not inclined to carp. "I shan't come out to the carriage, Catherine: can't

76

think why Berrington had to invite the Dauntry gal," he interposed, revealing naïvely that Melissa was his prime reason for not descending to the chaise. "I only hope you don't object to such a rattle for a companion at this time, eh?"

"Not the least in the world," she told him with fervour.

"Good girl! All's right and tight, then. Now, you're not to fret yourself to fiddlestrings over writing billets to me. Berrington will inform me himself of when the betrothal announcement is to be made, and you may be sure I shall come down there for *that*. Goodbye, my dear." He motioned at her cheek, then drew back and nodded at his cousin. "Goodbye, Honora—and be careful of her."

He turned on his heel and strode back to his study, but not before Catherine had perceived the glint of tears in his eyes. She felt stricken afresh. However, the loaded carriage now awaited them, and there was no time for further reflection on the Banker's odd, deep nature before she was borne away from him.

In contrast to herself, Melissa was bedecked just as entrancingly as the resolution of a scheming mother, and the skills of an experienced dresser, could between them contrive: from the frothy lime-green ostrich plumes of her straw bonnet to the exquisitely embroidered and flounced primrose muslin dress, under a cottage mantle of yellow silk, she looked every inch the young lady who was about to become affianced; whereas, when Catherine took her place beside her, she gave every appearance of a mere dependant upon this Vision.

In fact Lady Olivia's actual dependant, Miss

Acton, who was seated opposite the girls with Mrs Wilby, so far forgot herself as to give an audible snort of disgust when Catherine joined them. Had there been any more travellers, the dresser would have found herself banished to the rumble seat outside, but as it was she felt herself distinctly superior to the pair of dowds who had just boarded. A certain confidence began to settle over her sharp features, and she replied shortly and aloofly when the newcomers addressed her.

Catherine, in her over-wrought state, was immediately sensible of the dresser's hostility; on top of everything else it made her feel like weeping for her wretched aunt and herself. But Melissa's gaiety and high spirits were well able to surmount every other cross-current of feeling in the closed carriage; indeed, Catherine thought that she might be completely unaware of them.

Her light chatter saw them off the stones of London and through the turnpike at New Cross. She then kindly asked the dresser how she went on: "For she is the most abominably queasy traveller, are you not, Acton?"

Not even a monosyllable was answered to this tender inquiry from her young mistress: she closed her malevolent eyes and kept them so until Dartford was reached, while Mrs Wilby stared out of the window.

Presently Melissa delved into the pocket in the lining of the chaise and drew forth a copy of the *Lady's Magazine*. With a measuring look at Catherine's pale face, she handed it to her and said: "*This* will distract you."

Mrs Wilby's professional eye was shifted alertly from the passing scene by these words; but when she saw the object in question was not some unimproving novel as she had feared, she smiled vaguely at the girls and resumed her window gazing.

"Do pray look at the fashions on page 290," Melissa insisted, with a nudge.

Catherine complied in a half-hearted way, and then nearly dropped the magazine as a note fell from it on to her lap.

"Isn't that the most tonnish fan you ever saw?" Melissa made a show of pointing to the fashion plate with her dainty kid-gloved hand, while in fact ensuring that the piece of paper was not revealed to Mrs Wilby. "Well, stupid *read what it says!*" she whispered intensely.

Catherine had little difficulty in deciphering her friend's round clear script. Its message was brief and to the point. 'Upon arrival at our Destination you are to succumb to the Rigours of the Journey, and must seek your bed at once. In this Manner you might keep your Room for the first day or more.' Apart from the message itself, the final words 'Destroy this' were printed dramatically at the bottom of the paper. She looked in dumbfounded fashion at her companion, who was now saying brightly: "And it is a stunning gown, is it not?" Another covert nudge elicited the stammering reply:

"Yes—oh, yes! Very nice."

"No, not *nice,* Catherine, dear—such an insipid word," observed Mrs Wilby, startling them both: they had supposed their exchange was not audible above the rock and clatter of the chaise. Hastily Catherine turned the page, obliterating the note, then remained for some little time staring in sightless comtemplation of the periodical's monthly offering of verse now open before her.

The horses were changed at the Bull Inn at Dartford, where they alighted themselves to partake of some light refreshment. None of the passengers discovered much appetite for more than a sip or two of coffee; although Miss Acton made a recovery from her vaunted travel sickness and took rather more than a sip of fortifying spirituous liquor as well. Consequently, and to Honora Wilby's great satisfaction, that supercilious creature presently unbent to the point of snoring, in the most ungenteel fashion, for the remainder of the journey.

The interlude at the inn at least afforded the two girls an opportunity for an untrammelled talk. "So you will do it?" murmured Melissa as they walked back to the carriage.

"Yes, I suppose so."

By this time, in truth, she felt readier to take refuge in her room at the Challow as soon as she arrived, rather than straightway dash down Mr Berrington in the spirited style she had rehearsed. But she had no liking for the subterfuge that would be involved: however, this was as naught to the ever-nearer and more menacing presence of her suitor, which dictated her doubting answer for her.

"Excellent!" said Melissa robustly. "That means I might well sit by the Colonel at dinner in your place."

"Do you think he will be waiting to greet us when we arrive?"

"Not necessarily. Rosalind—that's his sister— acts hostess for him, you know. As like as not he'll be about the estate with his friends, or perhaps on an expedition somewhere." She uttered a careless giggle. "Rosalind *is* a bit terrifying, I suppose."

"Is she?" murmured Catherine faintly, beyond further alarms.

"Well, not really—but she is an ageing ape leader, and more than a shade oddish in her ways," Melissa said demolishingly. "But it's the Colonel *we're* interested in, and we shall meet him just before dinner—or I shall, that is."

Their steps had by now reached the carriage, where a complaining Mrs Wilby was being helped inside by the groom, while Miss Acton glassily regarded her. "Now Cathy—don't on any account forget to destroy that note," Melissa reminded her with a return to *sotto voce;* and then they, too were assisted to board the chaise and resumed their journey.

They stopped briefly at another Bull Inn, this time at Rochester, and then after crossing the River Medway the vehicle turned off the pike road towards the North Downs. Catherine was now alert for any promising-looking staging inns along the way, but as they continued to climb through the leafy lanes she was forced to conclude that the Dover Road, which had been left many miles behind, would afford the nearest of these; which was not encouraging should she be wishful to making an independent departure from Challow. However, she had brought sufficient funds, indeed all the money she possessed in the world—twenty guineas —in order to pay for such a precipitate flight if need be. But as the chaise horses slowed their pace along the hilly, narrow roads her spirits sank to their very lowest ebb: she saw there was going to be little prospect of an easy escape from Challow, wherever it might be in this desolate country.

"I'm almost sure I recognize that enormous windmill," Melissa remarked presently. "I believe we were almost there—Acton will know. Acton, wake up!" Whereupon that handmaiden's knee was roughly shaken. "Tell me—are we not near our destination?"

The snores ceased as Acton, striving for dignity, adjusted her bonnet and looked out of the window. "Yes, miss, not far now: I spied that landmark myself, a half mile back," she said coolly.

About that same distance further on they were halted before tall lodge gates, which were opened with despatch. *Now there is no escape,* Catherine told herself, leaning back on the squabs to hide herself from sight until the last possible moment.

Melissa chose this point to say, in deliberate accents: "You look monstrously pale, Cathy—are you not well?" And, being still in doubt of her friend's attentiveness to the plan she had devised for her, she gave her a sharp reminding kick.

"Oh!—er, yes—I do have the headache: I fear I have not stood out the journey very well." Which was by now true enough, though she still hated to draw her aunt's expert attention.

Sure enough, that lady's gaze was at once removed from the parkland to fix alertly upon her wan charge. However she was not unduly perturbed, merely saying: "Mm—just an attack of the nerves, I collect. I should have anticipated it. . . ." She reached under the seat for a small dressing case and passed a vinaigrette across to Catherine. "That will serve for the present—but dinner is all you need, my girl."

To her surprise, this cheerful opinion drew an agitated response from both girls.

"But couldn't I rather——?"

"Oh, stuff, ma'am! Shouldn't she——?"

"—request to keep my room until I feel more recruited? I know I just cannot face *anyone* at the moment," Catherine declared, without the slightest need for dissimulation.

Mrs Wilby pursed her lips and stared at her; in fact all the other occupants of the carriage then subjected her to a severe scrutiny.

"She does look awful," said Melissa at last, in a thrilling whisper.

"Yes! And principally because she is wearing those deplorable clothes!" the hard-pressed chaperon burst forth. "How else can she look but awful?—but she wouldn't listen to a word I said. Heaven preserve us!—whoever heard of *dun brown* for an occasion of this nature?"

After this passionate heart-cry, Miss Acton began to regard Honora Wilby with a first glimmering of respect. She had indeed uttered a few supporting words when the chaise lurched clumsily to a stop, tossing Mrs Wilby and the dresser into each other's arms as though in prompt celebration of their new-found accord.

Immediately a kind of restrained pandemonium broke out amongst the majority inside the carriage.

"We're here! See the great portico, Cathy! Oh, let me get down!" cried Melissa, regaining her balance with a hand already on the door.

"Not till I've tied that mantle ribbon, you don't," avowed the dresser, turning her firmly around again to face her.

"Cathy—pluck up, for pity's sake! *Remember what we are about!*" Mrs Wilby enjoined in a voice of entreaty.

Catherine alone was silent, her large grey eyes looking out wretchedly at the house. They had drawn up at the foot of broad stone steps flanked by plinths supporting entwined heraldic beasts. A tall footman in blue livery, accompanied by the butler, were descending the seemingly endlessly flight towards the drive. At the top of the steps was a heavy portico shielding the main entrance. The whole put her in mind of the newly-built Covent Garden theatre, and seemed more like a temple than a house: fitting, indeed, since she felt distinctly more like a human sacrifice than a guest. . . .

"Catherine!" came Mrs Wilby's harried tones again. "I beg of you, prepare yourself to step down."

She alighted before Melissa; to the vexation of them both. By the time that they had made themselves known to the butler, and Miss Acton had been driven on to the servants' entrance, another figure came stepping down to greet them; and she knew with a sudden chill that it was He.

"Cathy," murmured Melissa between a clenched-teeth smile of frustration. "I *thought* we settled that you were to throw a spasm!"

But no amount of such prompting could now distract her attention from this odious man who had so disrupted her peaceful life. She had to admit that he looked quite as tall and magisterial as she remembered him, even when he had arrived finally on their own level, but she had never seen him before except in the black evening dress he

invaribly wore in town. Now, clad in informal garb
of light green riding coat and cream breeches, he
looked a little younger than she recalled, in spite of
the greying wings on the dark wiry hair—although
his actual age was still difficult to hazard. He
could, she supposed, be considered handsome, for
his features were regular and without any notice-
able blemish. Lines were deeply etched on his
lean cheeks, and the brows, thick and straight,
lent him a slightly scowling appearance which
she had hitherto attributed to his actual expression. A powerful-looking chin completed a strong,
domineering countenance. His eyes had certainly
lost none of their *hauteur* as they moved over his
motley trio of guests; though their gaze was a
shade more bearable without the quizzing glass,
she decided.

He made himself known first to Mrs Wilby;
rendered a little at a loss by the deep curtsy of
obeisance which the older woman dropped him,
and then turned to the young pair.

"Servant, ma'am," he addressed Melissa, his
bow eliciting a most dazzling but somehow disregarded smile from her. "Miss Ebford—I welcome
you to Challow—but stay! I can see now you are
quite knocked up by your journey, and so I shall
not trouble you with formalities at this present.
Come, first meet my sister, who will show you
straightway to your room, where you may rest for
as long as you wish. Oh, and should you feel
disinclined to take dinner with us, it will be quite
understood."

Melissa's smile broadened out once again at
this juncture, until she heard her friend saying
unaccountably: "No, sir, I'm sure I shall be well

enough recovered after a short rest. The journey was a trifle fatiguing, this is all."

Mrs Wilby was plainly and vastly relieved at this belated show of good sense, but Melissa's complexion darkened ominously as they followed their host up the steps.

Rosalind Berrington now awaited them between the columns of the porch: a Junoesque figure of scarcely less impressive stature than her brother, she looked well cast as the goddess of the temple, thought Catherine; still in fanciful vein about the house. Miss Berrington herself seemed bent on playing that role to the full by wearing a simple gown of white classical draperies, not altogether suited to a lady of her build or years. Catherine saw that the features she shared with her brother were predictably over-strong for a female; as was her voice.

"Delighted to know you," she boomed down at Mrs Wilby, and enfolding her hand in a tight though careless grip. "*Ah!*—and my *dear* Miss Ebford!" And Melissa, with no time to be startled, found herself drawn up the final step and into a formal embrace.

"Er, no, Ros," her brother interposed, "that is Miss Dauntry—this is Miss Ebford."

"Oh," merely said Miss Berrington; yet conveying in the one syllable a summary of her views on that circumstance which was plain to them all.

"Miss Ebford is tired from the journey and wishful to be shown upstairs without delay," Mr Berrington said harshly at the end of the awkward pause which had been engendered. "When you have seen all our visitors in, perhaps you will come to me in the Salon." His face, which had grown particularly stern as he spoke, became almost kindly as he took his leave of them. "I trust you will find everything to your liking and soon feel refreshed. Until dinner, then."

The heels of his riding boots struck on the marble floor as he strode off; a sound which was soon augmented by Rosalind's resonant voice as she shepherded the trio of newcomers towards the stairway. He smiled, despite the anger which still filled him over her behaviour: he was always put irresistibly in mind of the parade ground when Ros took audible command of his household.

He prowled impatiently about the Salon, waiting for her, and pondering the curious fact that since his return from the Peninsula she had given every sign of regarding him almost as an intruder here. The years of his absence had given her an illusion of reigning supreme, and he had not begrudged her that, but now it was proving difficult for him to order things his own way without an uncomfortable degree of domestic friction. As a busy man of affairs, obliged to entertain a good deal, it was essential that he should have a competent hostess to stand beside him; but Rosalind was really too efficient for his taste; and he had known before today that she had a decided turn for alarming and browbeating any guests who lacked her own robustness, whether they were of one sex or the other.

Yes, aside from all other considerations, it was clearly high time for him to take a wife; a course he had embarked upon in the full knowledge that his sister was unlikely to approve the step—to put it at its mildest. That she would decide to dislike his choice he had also expected; but not that she would express herself so blatantly. It was the outside of enough—and so he would tell her. . . .

"Yes, Lucian, what is it you want?" she called out to him from the doorway, upon entering the Salon a few minutes later. She stood there, arms akimbo, and regarding him with a certain knowingness which irritated him afresh.

He beckoned from his stance by the fireplace. "Do you come in—properly—since I have no wish to discuss with you at ten yards distance."

'Oh, I haven't the time to pluck a crow with you now." And she remained stubbornly by the big door, toying with its swans-neck handle.

"Why should you think that was my intention?"

"Because it very often is!" she said with a sharp crack of laughter, and evidently unbending a trifle as she walked forward a few paces in stately fashion, and with an air of great forbearance.

"Be that as it may, what is it that makes such onerous demands on your time at the moment? We still have only four guests under our roof, I collect, and of them Felix scarcely counts, as he is forever roaming the grounds seeking inspiration— or whatever it is he does."

"The other three are like to make up for *that*," she told him forcefully. "First, I have to see cook and tell him to put dinner back an hour—tho' whether the sickly one will be able to eat by then I beg leave to doubt."

This further disparagement of his Intended drew a withering glower upon her which had faced down many an errant Dragoon; but it left Miss Berrington quite unmoved. His ire rose.

"You will refer to my future wife by her name, if you please," he said in his severest manner. "And

I was not pleased by your childish display earlier, I might add. You knew full well who Miss Dauntry was." He gave a long sigh, then continued with less heat: "Now, is it wholly necessary to keep dinner back till seven? That would be bound to throw everyone out, and at all events I have no desire to inflict a formal dinner on Miss Ebford before she is ready for it: as for the others, they're sure to be sharp-set long before then after a day of travelling."

"It's too late to alter it now, I have told them seven," she said calmly, seating herself in an old-fashioned bergère chair.

"Well, I wish you had not! Felix, for one, will not know of the change and will soon be under my feet at a time when I least want him there—and I shudder to think what an hour's respite will do to his voracious appetite!"

"The poor lamb needs feeding up," she said with indulgence. He was aware that she had a soft spot for the fragile-looking youth under discussion, the son of their elder sister; though he himself had long designated him a scheming wastrel. However, for his own reasons he was inclined to be well-disposed towards him at the moment and therefore he returned no answer.

"Lucian—I will be frank," she said suddenly and ominously, "I am persuaded you *cannot* be serious in your scheme to wed one who makes such a lamentable figure. My dear, she is *quite*——"

He interrupted her very quietly but in a way that made her fall silent.

"Rosalind, I know you very well and that you are forever cutting up characters. It signifies nothing most of the time—but I do caution you to keep a curb on your tongue in this instance. Try for a little civility: and why leap to conclusions about the girl after one glance at a drab pelisse and a travel-worn complexion? I have quite resolved to take a wife, and, though it is not to be hoped you would agree, it is a sensible—nay, an *admirable* decision."

"To be sure it is!" she returned with seeming contrariness. "But I beg you will fix upon one who is worthy of yourself and the name Berrington, and has a dash of style and spirit—like Miss Dauntry! Not a——"

He turned swiftly towards her. "Ros—I have warned you. I have not the least desire to play the heavy brother but——"

"And nor am I cast in the mould of a downtrodden and crushed sister!" she retorted with her customary fullness of lung.

"Very true," he murmured wryly.

"And pray remember, I took charge here whilst you were away on your military adventures, at your request, and for that same, sole reason I have stayed since your return. As soon as there is another—hopefully a *fitting*—mistress of Challow, then I shall very willingly set up my own establishment! You seem forgetful that I have my independence from Papa and need want for nothing!"

"I do not dispute one word of that—although I cannot believe your duties here have been as onerous as you seem to claim. And certainly nothing you have done on my behalf gives you *carte blanche* to dash down the lady of my choice." He paused thoughtfully, and with a gleam of mischief lightening the sternness in his eyes. "Now I think of it—when that redoubtable Mr Broadstone had you in a string last year, you did not hear me speak of 'unfittingness', did you?—though, by God, I could have!"

At the recollection of that erstwhile admirer whom he had so cheaply alluded to, a dark flush suffused her face, emphasized by the snowy lace cap and unrelieved white of her dress. "No, you did not," she said slowly, searching in her mind for a riposte. "But then, I was clear-headed enough *through my own council* to give him his *congé*, was I not? It is my fervent hope you may do the same before it is too late!"

She rose triumphantly to her feet and made for the door. "Ros," he called after her, "you should know that I have quite resolved to wed Miss Ebford and that nothing can shake me in that. Good Lord, woman!—you can hardly accuse me of youthful impetuousness! You may choose your own course of action: either remain—which you are very welcome to do—until the wedding day, or throw any kind of rub in the way of it and take your departure at once, never to set foot here again. Do I make myself clear?"

She turned, stared hard at him for a moment, tossed her head, and then left without a word.

SEVEN

Catherine was lying on the bed with the curtains closed around her, while Melissa roamed restlessly about the apartment they were to share during their stay at Challow. Mrs Wilby, who had been allotted the adjoining dressing-room, had repaired there to take a nap, after administering lavender drops to her niece as a composer; although in the event Catherine was not being afforded much opportunity to sleep.

"I hope Acton doesn't gossip in the hall much longer," Melissa addressed her shrouded friend, after a string of other observations of a similar kind, none of which demanded more than an occasional murmur from Catherine in reply. "For I must have my crape and lamé dress made ready for dinner." She eyed the heap of portmanteaux, trunks and bandboxes with all the natural impatience of a soldier withheld from his Arms before the commencement of a strenuous campaign. "Still, I daresay she will condescend to come up soon—and dinner is not until seven. I *must* say I am astonished the Colonel has not seen to it that we were each given a room of our own. I cannot think what Mama would say if she knew. . . ."

Catherine, with her eyes firmly closed but still feeling only too awake, thought that the arrangement was hardly wonderful, since Melissa had invited herself and the house was probably overflowing with other guests. However, she too wished that they could be lodged apart. She wanted to plan what she should do now, but the incessant chatter prevented this. She could foresee endless embarrassments with Melissa and their host—and his sister!

A hostile relative was one factor she had not expected to find here. And Miss Berrington's antagonism towards her could not be in doubt after that reception. She wondered suddenly if she might not put this hostility to use in some way: for example, tell her she concurred absolutely with her own clear view that the match with her brother was undesirable in the extreme? But no; she fancied she would as lief face Mr Berrington himself on that subject as his alarming and trumpet-tongued relation. He himself had not appeared unduly intimidating from the little she had seen of him; but then, why should he, while he believed that all was proceeding smoothly as he wished?

Melissa's tiresome voice impinged again. "Oh, there's someone walking towards the house. . . ."

"Who?" said Catherine wearily.

"No one in particular—just a man. It must be one of the other guests."

The sudden studied indifference would have aroused Catherine's suspicions had she not been wholly engrossed in her own thoughts. These influenced her to the point where, for a wild moment, she wondered whether Christopher could have arrived already on some pretext or other to carry her away; but common sense soon dispelled this notion. "I wonder how many others there are?"

"Oh, dozens: there always are. And all of the First Rank."

In fact, the Colonel's house-parties were renowned for their rustic quaintness, as her mama put it. But Melissa now deemed it prudent to instil the maximum degree of apprehension in her friend so that she would be fearful even to venture from this room, for several days, if that were possible.

Still standing at the window, and drawing a long finger nail dreamily along the pile of the apricot draperies, she watched the progress of the young man below with close attention. There was little danger she would be observed by him: the window was deeply recessed and besides, he seemed oblivious of his surroundings. He carried a book under his arm, and the thought then came to her that he might well be the Colonel's poetical nephew, of whom she had heard but had never seen.

Her quick little mind began reviewing the possibilities this gentleman might introduce into the unfolding situation at Challow. She herself did not greatly care for the languishing, bookish type, but it occurred to her that he might serve admirably as a diversion for Catherine. However, before she embroidered the basic scheme in any way, she would first make his acquaintance and judge what manner of man he was. In the ordinary way, she was confident of her ability to bring all those of his sex and age around her thumb; but poets could be difficult. She remembered, with mortification, a versifier friend of Christopher's from Cambridge, who had qualified as one of her Total Failures: he had declaimed the Lord Byron by the hour, and looked through her as though she were not there.

In the merciful silence which accompanied these various reflections, Catherine endeavoured to make up her mind on the question of going down to dinner. Contrary to Melissa's intent in telling her there would be a large number of fellow guests, she found this encouraging in a way. She could not now believe that the at least punctilious Mr Berrington could mean to put her to the blush in front of a large company by any reference to his offer; and neither could he very well talk to her alone in those circumstances. But on the other hand, she would have to partner him in to dinner almost certainly, and that she shrank from as much as ever.

As if following her mind, Melissa then put her head around the bed curtains, dropping her voice to a whisper: "Of course you will not appear at dinner, since no one now expects you to?"

All at once Catherine's independent spirit rebelled: why should she be told how to go on by Melissa? She was quite capable of sending Mr Berrington to the rightabout without any assistance from her, she was tolerably sure. Whether this new surge of resolution sprang from sheer curiosity, or from the potent effects of lavender

drops on an empty stomach, she was less certain;
but when Mrs Wilby awoke she found that both
girls were dressed. They were also uncommonly
silent; Melissa having taken huff over her friend's
vexatious changeableness.

The chaperon retired briefly again to dress for
dinner herself, declining a quite friendly offer of
assistance from the dresser, who appeared to be in a
much better plight after her journey than could
reasonably have been expected. In fact Miss Acton
had found her spell in the housekeeper's room
most revivifying, having been very well looked
after there and also regaled with more information concerning the Family than her betters would
discover in a month.

Catherine had selected her simplest evening
dress: a robe of palest blue crape with tiny puff
sleeves, its only trimming being a dainty edging
of white silk rosettes to the shoulders, sleeves and
hem. For jewelry she wore a double row of white
satin beads, and she carried a fan of carved ivory.
What she had not calculated (and would have
been dismayed to know) was that the particular
shade of blue enhanced her eyes most fetchingly,
in Aunt Wilby's carefully unexpressed opinion.

Melissa's Pomona green tunic, over a dress of
white silk, also matched her eyes, but had been
chosen very differently: she had determined to
make a ravishing impression that night which
would win the battle for her in its opening skir-
mish. And with silver lamé ornamenting the skirt,
and the long sleeves ruched and beribboned, she
was indeed striking, thought Catherine; who noted
with appreciation this bold attempt to detach the
Colonel from herself at the outset. She did feel,

however, that the addition of an emerald neck-lace, bracelet and ear-drops, was painting the lily somewhat, and must surely risk being deemed *outré* at a gathering such as this. On that point she was unknowingly in full accord with the experienced Acton, who had stopped only just short of impudence in her efforts to dissuade her mistress from wearing the stones altogether.

Thus formidably attired, Melissa led the way when the time came at last for them to meet their fellow guests.

They were shown into a circular Salon to be received by their host, his sister, and the young man Melissa had already seen. A rather stiff silence pervaded the occasion: of the visiting trio, Catherine and Melissa were still exchanging no more than an infrequent monosyllable; while between the resident three, Rosalind Berrington had not addressed even as much as that to Lucian since their brangle earlier. Fortunately, however, the effect of this was dispelled by the nervous garrulity of Mrs Wilby and the easy charm of Mr Moreton-Frodsham.

When the latter was made known to the ladies as Mr Berrington's nephew, he startled them by greeting them in an overtly Gallic fashion. *"En-chanté!"* he declared resonantly as he kissed each hand, lingering an instant longer over Melissa's to plumb the depths of those green eyes.

Mrs Wilby, garrulous no longer, began to show signs of still greater unease. She had not a word of French at her command, and suddenly her chaperoning duties seemed likely to prove even more onerous than she had feared. First, she had suffered all this bother with Cathy; and now—as if that was not enough—a Foreign Fortune-hunter. . . .

However, even Aunt Wilby soon came to realize that Mr Moreton-Frodsham was in fact as English as anyone else present. His manner might be flamboyant but his dress was quite unexceptionable; only the eye of a connoisseur would have detected the subtle difference between the cut of his coat and the set of his cravat, and those same garments upon his uncle standing beside him. Both wore white waistcoat, black pantaloons with striped silk stockings, and preferred Mr Brummell's choice of a blue coat for evening.

This sartorial coincidence was no happy accident: Felix Moreton-Frodsham was a cunning young man who devoted a good deal of his time to devising ways of extracting funds from the well-breeched brother of his widowed parent. When he was not at Challow his style of dress had been described, even by his contemporaries, as 'rather of the ratherest', and, whatever his motives, Lucian could only be grateful that such creations were never inflicted upon him. The only present hint of his poetic leanings was in his golden locks, which were allowed to curl over his collar most unfashionably.

Lucian now rallied him over his Continental demeanour. "If you fail to understand him, he has only himself to blame!—he is merely passing through what I collect is the modern tendency of being enamoured of everything French."

This was said with a certain good-natured contempt, and it was not allowed to go unchallenged by Felix. "That, uncle, is a gross calumny! No gentleman's education can be thought complete

until he has been to Paris—and for the *whole of
my life* this has been denied me, due to Boney and
his war!" He waved both his arms in a French
flourish. "Now it is *still more* insupportable—
since there is Peace, and everyone who is anyone
is flocking once again to the Seat of all Culture!"

"But you are not?" Melissa said softly; she found
this passionate creature vastly more intriguing
than the Byronic youth who had formed her original opinion of poets.

He shrugged, and jutted his lower lip. *"Peut-
être?* Who knows?" he murmured with an air of
high tragedy.

Lucian here favoured his nephew with another
glance that was half-amused, half exasperated,
and Catherine, who had been grateful for this
diversion from herself, saw with surprise that Mr
Berrington had a very expressive face when the
frown was relaxed; his eyes held a touch of humour
that she had not suspected. Nonetheless, he was
not a man she looked forward to thwarting, having a strong presentiment that any amusement in
the matter might well be at her own expense.

He was saying now in sardonic tones: "Sometimes it crosses my mind that the sole reason I am
blessed with Felix's delightful company is because
of the concidence that Challow stands some fifty
miles nearer to his 'seat of culture' than does his
mother's house, across the Thames in Essex: that
must be why he feels a shade closer to his goal
here than when under her roof."

Felix's fair complexion heightened at this
home-thrust, but the remark had its intended
effect. Paris was not mentioned again, or, at all
events, not until afterwards when they walked

into dinner and the poet found himself placed fortuitously next to Melissa.

After witnessing this public, albeit humane routing of Mr Frodsham, Catherine's abiding fear, that her betrothal might be aired before the company, returned in full measure. But, once Lucian had satisfied himself that all the travellers were restored from their journey—and, to her relief, he accomplished that without making her feel particular—he launched into a detailed history of his house, in response to a merely formal question from Mrs Wilby.

"Yes, it is rather unusual, is it not: tho' not unique by any means. My late father, when he returned from the army, began another campaign of touring the countryside in search of the style of home he was wishful to build. At that time he lived in a snug enough place near here—and, as it happpened, did not need to pass beyond the county boundary to discover his perfect model: Mereworth Castle." He sighed, and his lips puckered humorously again.

"Oh, enchanting! I *did* think he had perhaps taken Lord Burlington's villa at Chiswick in liking," Mrs Wilby said brightly.

"He might equally well have done," he agreed with a laugh. "For it is very similar again. Neither edifice, in my view, is exactly habitable—or deserving of *enthusiastic* reproduction in your average slice of parkland. Oh, they brim with architectural worth, I don't doubt, but as residences for us nowadays they lack a certain——"

"*Je ne sais quoi?*" Felix neatly interposed.

Rosalind Berrington joined in the smiles only because it was her favourite nephew's riposte to the set-down he had received earlier, and she was quite straight-faced when she declared in her ringing voice: "I have always treasured this house in every way. Papa made an admirable choice and it stands a fitting memorial to him."

That this was merely a shaft at her out-of-favour brother, Lucian himself was well aware, and he did not deign to take up the challenge other than by a speaking glance to remind her of his warning.

The two girls had been almost silent listeners so far. Catherine was studying the unusual windowless circular room, its pale blue walls decorated with large and yet intricate white plaster reliefs, and the glazed dome above transmitting an astonishing amount of evening summer light. Indeed, this unusual feature engrossed Melissa's attention so greatly that the nearby figure of Mr Frodsham, hovering in readiness to lead her in, appeared to be quite ignored by her; making his expression grow quite anxious and tantalized.

Again Mrs Wilby made a diffident inquiry. "You were speaking of your father—would that be General Berrington, by chance, of India fame?"

Even Rosalind's black looks softened at this lucky hit, and Lucian said in surprise: "Yes, ma'am! How comes it that you know—that is to say, I am impressed by your comprehensive interests, be they in architecture or the army! But now to the prosaic matter of dinner."

Honora Wilby quite bridled with gratification, and began to hope that her stay at Challow might not prove such an ordeal after all; and her ward perceived very clearly that she herself was now the sole representative of her sex who remained immune to the 'dear Colonel's' charms.

By the conclusion of dinner, she was also sensible of the fact that at least her first evening was passing off well enough, and without any painful revelations being dragged from her forthwith. Apart from a brief attachment to Mr Berrington's arm, and being placed next to him at the table, she had been treated with all the impartiality that she could have desired. She was further relieved to find that despite Melissa's tales, apart from Mr Frodsham they were the sole guests; so when she finally did have to reject the offer, at least there would be no crowd of onlookers to be thrown into speculation by her abrupt departure from their midst.

One person who was unlikely to be rendered at all inconsolable by seeing the last of her, she would hazard, was Miss Berrington. For when they were awaiting the gentlemen in the drawing-room her bearing towards her had still been most pointed; her presence had been largely ignored while she conducted what was evidently intended as an exclusive cose with Melissa, in the main upon the subject of her nephew.

Meanwhile, that young gentleman was waxing loquacious, whilst Lucian frowned into his brandy glass.

". . . only right I should thank you for being such a Trojan over this present visit of mine, sir— 'specially, damme, when you've other guests. Funny to think I only expected to stay one night! Appreciate it no end—but never fear, I'll cut my stick tomorrow. Ain't this your best cognac wheeled out, too?" He held up his glass to the candle-shine, subjecting its contents to what he trusted might pass for a profound examination. *"Merveilleux!—* oh—sorry, Uncle!"

"Qu'importe?" Lucian responded good-naturedly. In truth he was glad to make amends for roasting the lad earlier. "If that is the correct expression."

"Tell the truth, sir, I ain't yet quite a Nonesuch with the lingo meself," the younger man said in a rare burst of frankness. "Wish the deuce I was— gives a fellow a ton nothing else can." Whereupon he checked, looking in apprehensive fashion at his very English uncle. "Shan't go on any more about that, though: know you deem it a dead bore!"

Lucian laughed. "You're an impressionable young whipper-snapper! *Maintenant, mon enfant— cartes sur table, s'il vous plaît!* You came here *exprès* to have me frank a Paris spree, *n'est ce pas?"*

"God, no!—dash it!—came to see you, Uncle!" Felix's face had turned pink at this tasteless realism on the part of his relative.

"Oh: you must forgive me, I misread the case. It's a pity, though," Lucian mused on to himself, "for it occurs to me that if you'd been willing to remain here for a few days more, I think I might then have been able to see my way to donating to that worthy cause—say five hundred?"

Felix ran a hand through his golden curls and gasped for a moment like a landed fish. "You're saying you'd tip over a *monkey* to me if I'm willin' to stay?" Recovering his dignity a little, he stuttered: "Lord, sir, you don't have to bribe a fellow to stay on here—not with some of the most delectable companions I've seen in many a long day!"

"That is just the point—I would want you to

squire one of the ladies you have just met. You see, it is a shade awkward for me to preside over four females until such time as the rest of the house party arrives."

His nephew was puzzled, though obviously disinclined to cast any sort of a rub in the way of the main proposition that had been put to him, merely remarking: "Then why the devil—er, why did you have 'em down early, eh?"

"I didn't, altogether. The problematical one invited herself. So you see your visit is quite timely—if you could consent to stay."

"If this don't beat the Dutch! Of course I'll stay, and you don't have to *pay* me! Dammit, I'd rather you didn't! Well," he amended hastily, "that is, a fellow don't like to feel he has to be bought to tolerate a female's society, y'know."

"I think that most praiseworthy general principle might depend, in practice, on the female in question, don't you?" his uncle replied in the odd tone he sometimes used, when a fellow never quite knew if he was bamming you or not. "However, Felix, I take your point, and of course if you don't wish to——"

"Forgive me interrupting, sir, but might I know which lady we're discussin'?" Felix's smooth brow had momentarily assumed as mature a furrow as his uncle's, for if there was some catch in all this, he felt it was high time he discovered it. Fellows rarely got monkeys for nothing, in his experience.

"Miss Dauntry is the damsel I want you to keep entertained and out of mischief for me," Lucian told him, watching the frown vanish with almost comical speed; he had guessed Melissa's style of beauty would appeal to the boy. "It goes without saying, of course, that you will not step beyond the line of what is pleasing. I am on good terms with both the young lady and her mother," he added with emphasis.

Felix looked greatly affronted. "Beyond what's pleasing? Devil a bit! Oh, rest easy on that head, Uncle."

"I shall—unless you give me cause to disturb your own ease. Lady Olivia's daughter is impetuous, unattached to the best of my knowledge, and must I fear be described as a flirt of the first order," Lucian cautioned him. "So you see, your well-rewarded task may have its hazards, after all."

"Yes, sir," acknowledged his nephew with a cheerful grin.

"But as regards Miss Ebford—you would poach that preserve at your peril. Do I make myself clear?"

Felix eyed him dubiously for a moment, but decided he couldn't mean what he had first thought he meant: no, a schoolroom miss like that could never make an April gentleman out of an old stager like Berrington. He said again, but with rather less assurance: "Yes, sir."

"Good. Now, as to that other little matter—the Crindles have formed the intention of going over to Paris as soon as the celebration fever has died down a little. I'm persuaded they would gladly give an eye to your welfare over there. And I can provide other introductions, I daresay, which should ease your path. But I do this," he added severely, seeing the glowing face before him, "very largely for the sake of your long-suffering mama. Amelia has difficulties enough, Lord knows, with your three sisters to rear in a father's absence, without being driven to distraction by your constant Paris refrain. No!—don't seek to deny it! I am perfectly sure you must have 'just happened' to mention your French sojourn at home."

"Well, I might have, y'know," Felix allowed with a disarming smile. "But I've got to spit this out, sir—I'm overwhelmed by your generosity! The deuce of it is, I don't know how I'm ever to repay you."

"By not falling into any scrapes when you are abroad," returned Lucian promptly, "*and* by conducting yourself in an exemplary fashion whilst you are here. Which reminds me—the ladies must have given us up."

EIGHT

As Catherine suffered her aunt to put up her hair in curl-papers that first night at Challow, under the frankly pitying gaze of Melissa, her mood was, if possible, even more desponding.

For while Melissa had made not a jot of discernible progress in her official task of captivating their host, that could not be said apropos of his Frenchified nephew, she reflected wryly. However, this lack of support came as no great surprise to her: she had, after all, defied Melissa by appearing at dinner, which had caused pique in that fickle quarter. That aside, Lady Olivia's scheme, never wholly convincing, now seemed both outrageous and implausible here on the Colonel's home ground.

She was clearly going to be compelled to face up squarely to the situation herself, and inform him of her feelings at the very next opportunity. Reaching this decision bestowed a measure of composure upon her and, in spite of Melissa's indefatigable chatter, she fell asleep surprisingly quickly that night.

In the morning the new arrivals partook of a late and leisurely breakfast in their apartment, all three of them finally sallying forth together in search of their formidable hostess. Mrs Wilby was anxious that they should attend church, and when they were shown into Miss Berrington's dressing-room this was broached almost at once.

But it seemed the proposal did not hold a strong appeal for that lady. "Oh—yes," she said, in tones which indicated that Sunday church was deemed a rather Gothic notion at Challow, "if you are really wishful to attend I will tell Lucian, and give orders for a carriage to be brought round." And she eyed them bleakly, as if they were sinners well beyond such simple redemption.

"If it is in any degree inconvenient——" Honora Wilby began unhappily.

"Of course it is not," came the cold response. "Why should you think so?—my brother desires that everything should be done for your comfort." This was said in such a way as to doubt his sanity, but that there was no help for it. She reached for the bell-pull. "The carriage will be ready to leave within the half hour. I would advise you to go and dress now."

There was no mistaking the note of dismissal, and they left her feeling more chastened by the brief encounter than was at all likely from any subsequent sermon.

Lucian was crossing the hall as they emerged.

"Ah, good morning!" he called up to them in cheerful fashion. "I was wondering if I might count on your company to church this morning?" Mrs Wilby saying that he might, he continued: "Splendid! You know, it is a rare thing for the Berrington pew to sport such an attractive bevy of worshippers." His eyes fixed Catherine's as he said this, and it occurred to her then that this was to be her introduction to local society and the villagers; hence, no doubt, his own enthusiasm and Rosalind's disfavour. She was sharply aware now that every passing moment where she lacked either the courage or the ingenuity to reject his suit, only drew her the more deeply into the net.

But then, suddenly, she was presented with just that opportunity. When they were moving away from him along the passage he called after her: "Oh, Miss Ebford, I would appreciate a word with you, if I may?" And numbly she went down to him.

Lucian, being already dressed for church, had reverted to an imposing black tail-coat and pantaloons; presenting much the same dour figure Catherine remembered from their London meeting. She quailed, wondering what he would now say, though fiercely resolved to return him an honest answer. Unfortunately, though, he did not lead her into the privacy of a room but remained standing in the hall.

"I think I may owe you an apology," he began, "for not providing you with your own apartment. Shabby hospitality indeed, eh?—only I was given to understand you had expressed a most particular wish to have your friend at your side." And he seemed to convey just a hint of surprise at this desire by his intonation.

"What? Yes, I did!" she said impatiently, her mind still set on the more important question than her physical comfort. "We are all very content, I do assure you, sir."

"Well then, that disposes of that, at least." He smiled at her in a way that was kindly, but something very much more as well. The unexpectedness of it took her breath away, and effectively scattered all her thoughts and firm intentions. "Ah—I see Machin there—pray excuse me, I must see that arrangements for the Service are put in hand, for we shall be leaving shortly. Until then, my dear!"

His long-legged military stride bore him away from her and over to the butler in seconds, and she was left staring in hopeless frustration across the echoing hall, quite bereft herself for the moment of the power to walk.

When at last she did gain her room once more, Melissa was all agog.

"Well—what did he say? Cathy, have you told him now?" She spoke in whispers since Honora was then barely out of earshot.

"No, it was nothing at all," she muttered in an equally low voice, going over to her aunt. "I'll wear my blue pelisse for church," she told her dully.

Mrs Wilby's look of staunch optimism faded; she thought her niece was still being unaccountable over the vexed question of her dress. "Not, surely, with your rosebud muslin?—it must be the pink silk spencer—at least, *most* people would say so!"

"Yes . . . that was what I meant, of course, dear Aunt."

Honora thereupon shook her head over her most speakingly, and Catherine continued in like blank-minded fashion until the three of them were descending the endless stone steps from the house to where a barouche was drawn up. Mr Berrington was already on the box, evidently intending to drive the pair of shafted black roans himself.

"I fear it may be a tight squeeze for you all," he called down apologetically as the footman moved forward to hand in Mrs Wilby.

"Not in the least—for I will take the forward seat," proposed Melissa, tossing a dazzling smile to the driver as she spoke, "and then we may all be comfortable!" Upon being thanked effusively for this gesture of self-sacrifice in taking what was properly a servant's place, she sat facing her two companions with an expression of befitting saintliness, all the way to church.

But if, as Catherine suspected, her friend was now making a belated push to draw Mr Berrington's attentions, she could have told her that she was wasting her time; there had been no mistaking the look of ardour he had given her back in the house. That his suit emanated from real attachment had never even crossed her mind, and, of course, made the task of rejecting it yet more distasteful while being still more necessary.

However, as their group walked into the little church she told herself stoutly that one warm glance could scarcely be said to change anything; she merely had to avoid his direct gaze as much as possible until his own sensibility made him desist. But although she employed this device forthwith, nevertheless she was aware that he was now treating her with the particular deference which his pride saw as due to the future Mrs Berrington. He guided her into the family pew, and sat by her side pointing out all the notable figures in the congregation; and, although she focued rigidly upon the parson throughout the Service, it proved next to impossible for her not to acknowledge her companion's existence when he retrieved her abandoned parasol as they rose to leave. Her cheeks flamed as his eyes again held hers—and again conveyed that undeniable message.

Lord, she thought: she just *had* to speak to him and dispel this, but her battered spirits were now quite unequal to that prospect. For he was no longer the cold, heartless monster she had built up in her consciousness as 'Mr Berrington': he was a real, forceful person, and she could not imagine herself successfully rejecting him as she had planned to. No, she would now rather quit Challow without a word, she decided; and naturally at the first possible moment, although by what means she was still quite at a loss to know. . . .

Her character differed in that respect very greatly from that of Lady Olivia. Her ladyship was never left at a loss for very long when it came to deliberating possible courses of action. Once Melissa had departed for Challow, she had become beset with doubts that that young lady's only burgeoning powers of intrigue were sufficient to sway the Colonel. Being constitutionally unable to leave events to take their course, she had taken the step of inviting Lord Ebford to dinner; and, as one of her more longstanding aims was to furnish that gentleman with a wife, the only other guest at her board was the widowed Countess of Honley.

Lord Ebford had become accustomed, over the last few months, to seeing this meek and good-natured lady at Portland Street; and, as she had replaced another widowed lady of slightly more mature years, who had for a time been an equally familiar fellow guest, he had assumed that Lady Olivia had a preternaturally tender heart towards the bereaved. In fact the elder lady selected for him had had the temerity to pledge herself else-where before the relationship with Ebford could ripen. The more eligible—and, she felt, more reliable—Lady Honley had received her first invi-tation card as soon as she had put off her blacks, almost a year ago.

Christopher Dauntry, who with his father made up the small party, was now experiencing an ever-increasing burden of guilt over Catherine. He was gloomily convinced that a stouter-hearted fellow than he would have snatched her from her predicament before now; and yet he was still bereft of a single idea as to how to further that end in a conformable style. But he was usually taci-turn and so this preoccupation went quite unno-ticed; the more so since his pallid parent was soon well-launched into one of his cheery monologues.

Lady Honley listened to him, her sweet and pretty face surrounded with a halo of fine though slightly fading blonde hair, and animated with the most punctilious interest and attention. Chris-topher had on numerous occasions marvelled at her patience with his parent's fiddlestick tongue, and so thought nothing of it this time but allowed his attention to drift away from them.

He noticed out of the corner of his eye that his mother had guided the Banker to the far side of the largest aviary in the room. After a brief inspection of some new feathered inmates, their heads were soon together in earnest discourse. He wished he could eavesdrop, knowing that his mother sometimes chose to discuss important matters from that vantage point, secure in the knowledge that any presence near the big cage would incite its occupants to a clamour that would drown out anything that was said to the ears of the rest of the room.

"You must be feeling pleased, dear George," she said loudly, after an opening reference to Princess Charlotte's engagement to the Prince of Orange, "that your little Cathy is so much more happily settled." She tapped him on the arm with her fan and turned her famous sparkling blue gaze fully upon him. "I don't scruple to say that you stole a march on me with your capture of the Colonel—it came like a thunderbolt that I was to lose one of my charges so soon to matrimony."

They made an impressive pair, both tall and slim, and Lord Ebford was only just able to look down upon her and say in his driest manner: "You of all people, ma'am, must apprehend that it wouldn't serve for one in my position to blazon his affairs abroad before the seal is set on an agreement." At which he gave a slight token smile to show awareness of his own pomposity, before continuing: "Once it was, you had the news posthaste, I collect?"

"Yes indeed: she came straightway to tell me." She was resolved to ignore the imputation that she could not be trusted with his confidence, but could not forbear from adding: "And I hope I may depend on you to inform me *just as soon* as you have a settled date for the betrothal?"

"Yes, yes," he said testily. "I'm in expectation of a letter from Kent on that very subject. The journeys down went off without mishap, you say?"

"Entirely. My coachman returned late last night with the vehicle intact, and not even a lamed horse." This exchange was not proceeding in quite the way she had intended, and, perceiving that his lordship was casting progressively bleak glances down his patrician nose at the new and clamorous Java sparrows, she came bluntly to the point. "While we speak of Catherine and the Colonel, I own it does excite my astonishment that he should be happy to take a wife of unknown breeding—whatever lustre your connexion adds to her standing."

Because of the birdsong accompaniment it could not be said that there was silence between them, although Lord Ebford eyed her deliberately for some time before replying. Braced for an admonition, she ran her fan airily along the bars of the cage, though secretly a little fearful at what she had said to him.

But he merely shrugged. "You are in the right of it, of course. A man of Berrington's order would never have offered for a nobody."

At once her fan ceased teasing the birds. "And so?" she prompted with bald curiosity.

"Well, I can see no harm in your knowing, now everything is brought to a conclusion," he said judiciously. "The fact is, she is my niece—my late brother's child." Seeing the interest in her features, he began to regret this disclosure and added in his most quelling way: "You will oblige me by not uttering a word of this to a soul. Catherine herself is as yet in ignorance, and it is my firm intention to tell her *myself,* Olivia, when I deem the time is ripe."

"But of course! Oh, your little secret is safe enough with me, depend on it." And, having gathered a harvest rather beyond her expectations, she quite soon afterwards led the Banker back to the Countess, the irrepressibly cheerful William, and her subdued son.

She was as good as her word, having no intention of divulging what he had told her to anyone; though it was only natural for her to attempt to make some use of it for her own ends. At first, though, even she was at a stand to see how it could be exploited; conscious that it had effectively removed the central obstacle to Catherine's eligibility for the Colonel.

But, having faced that disagreeable fact, it did not take her ladyship very long to conclude that the girl had now also been rendered a trifle more attractive as their own daughter-in-law. Ebford had not mentioned the boy, Benjamin, but there seemed little doubt from their likeness that they were indeed brother and sister. She felt tolerably safe in assuming the boy must be his nephew, and, therefore, might be the next heir to the barony. If that were so, Ebford seemed bent upon denying him his inheritance—through pique that he had run off? It was curious, in that event, that the Banker had not re-married and secured the line with his own son.

Thoughtfully, she made a mental note to redouble her efforts with the widowed Countess. For one wild moment she even pictured Melissa in the role of Lady Ebford, but dismissed this reluctantly as lacking practicality at this stage; but later, perhaps, if all else failed?

The curve of her mouth slowly increased as she realized the many ramifications which might spread from one small nugget of information. It was a further pleasure to her to know that she was Ebford's confidante in the matter, especially following his earlier secretiveness.

"Christopher, dear," she hailed her first-born on the following evening, when William was at Brooks's. "You know, it does grieve me to see you so blue-devilled—and at your age, too!"

His eyes rose above the newspaper he held in his hand, but had not been reading. "Oh? What makes you say so?" he returned cautiously, a little unnerved by this maternal solicitude.

"Come, you can't flummery your own mother, you know! It's very plain you are as anxious about that poor girl as I am myself."

He flushed beneath his thatch of auburn hair, and wriggled a little in his seat at her tone of cloying concern. More cautiously still, he allowed: "I do own, Mama, that her—unhappy situation has crossed my mind from time to time."

"Of course it has! Why, I suppose I may claim to know my own son better than most! I hazard you are positively aching to do something to help her—are you not?"

"Well—that is—yes." Never fulsome in his own speech, on this occasion he found it nigh on impossible to pursue such a delicate matter in these terms. Also, he was bewildered by this departure from her previous attitude towards his association with Catherine, when she had always declined to discuss that with him. Neither had he yet wholly recovered from her deuced odd notion of hurling young Melly in Berrington's way.

Her ladyship, as cool as Christopher was made hot and flustered by this conversation, now fixed him with an experienced eye. "Chris, I must confess to you that I'm prey to a degree of misgiving as to my—ah—little hopes for Melissa's part in this affair."

Such direct poaching of his own thoughts shook him out of his reserve, just as she had intended. "So was I—from the outset!" he declared with feeling.

She raised her beautifully shaped eyebrows at him. "It was not so disastrous a scheme as all that, you know. But I don't deny its flaws—the principal of those being my own absence from Challow, since Melly can be a shade volatile, as of course you're aware."

He merely pursed his lips and said nothing to that; but she could not now have wished for a more attentive audience. It was passing through his mind that she might have formed some other 'little hope' for his sister; and one which would curl his liver worse still.

"Much may depend on the other guests who are down there," his parent was continuing. "I do not yet quite despair of Melissa's push to fix Berrington's interest, but I think we must remove Catherine before the announcement can be made and all be lost."

He gave a violent twitch. *"Remove? We?"* he echoed blankly.

She gave an impatient cluck. "Yes, it is the obvious thing! Before the end of the week you must post down there—oh, on some pretext of delivering something to Melly," she told him with a vague gesture. "Whilst there, you must speak to

Catherine, either alone or with your sister, and coax her to return with you—she'll need little persuasion, I'd vouch, for never have I seen such an unwilling bride."

Christopher's eyes were now as round as crown pieces. "Mama—consider what you are saying!" he cried in alarm. "—That I gain entrance to Berrington's house under false pretences, snatch his betrothed clandestinely, and place Catherine's reputation in the gravest jeopardy by compelling her to travel alone with me in the chaise to London! Unless, of course, you desire me to make off with Mrs Wilby as well, for chaperonage?" he concluded on a note of unwonted sarcasm.

"Lord!" she said, a little dashed. "The Wilby Woman—I had quite forgot her. No, she must not be involved."

"And Catherine's good name, ma'am?"

She shrugged, and made a cool recover. "—Need not be unduly sullied were she to wed you subsequently—indeed, the announcement could be made at once."

He swallowed. "Marry? Me? But—but I thought —I mean, I had gained the distinct impression that such an event would not be, well, much to your liking."

This was received with the blandest expression of sympathy from his parent. "I cannot think what gave you that idea, dearest boy! Why, William and I had distinct thoughts in that direction before Berrington spoilt your chances."

"Papa knows naught of this scheme, I'll go bail!"

"Ah, well, you know your father! In far less time than it takes to hire a chaise he would have let

121

slip to Ebford that you were on your way to Kent. But he will be as pleased as anyone when we succeed, I am perfectly sure I may speak for him in that."

"Look," Christopher told her earnestly, leaning forward so that his elbows pressed into his knees in a tense manner, "I make no promise that I'll undertake this freakish start, but, *if* I should, where do you propose I take Cathy?—for it is patent I cannot bring her here."

"Freakish, you call it!" she said with a toss of her head. "And have you rummaged up a better plan? No, of course she cannot be housed here, or anywhere in town, until the notice is in the *Gazette*. You must leave her with cousin Henrietta, near Bromley—that will lie in your way, if you return from Challow by Maidstone."

This inexorable resourcefulness was wearing him down. "Are you serious about this, Mama?" he inquired with very little hope. In truth he was slightly peeved not to have thought of their cousin himself as the source of a refuge, for he had to admit that the eccentric and wealthy spinster would serve such a purpose admirably.

"And why should I not be, pray?"

"I will tell you why not! Two excellent reasons: Mr Berrington and Lord Ebford. Dash it—they might both call me out at once—and I could scarcely blame them if they did!"

"I have considered that——" she began in all seriousness.

"Have you, by Jove!" he exploded.

"No, no, of course I don't mean that—what fustian you do talk sometimes! Neither of those gentlemen is in the least inclined to be hot at hand. As for Berrington, he will doubtless be relieved, privately, to have his reluctant bride so effortlessly removed, after suffering a few days of her sulky presence at Challow—for she is vastly sulky, you must know, Christopher! And without having to offer Ebford a direct affront, which he might well have shrunk from. Besides, he is not going to raise the breeze over such a scandal: he is a man of considerable standing and due for all manner of honours in the future, as all the world knows."

While far from convinced by this line of argument, he merely objected: "And his lordship? Even you cannot suppose he will look kindly on me as a son-in-law after snaring Berrington."

Her ladyship did not have a ready answer to this: she had, after all, spoken in much the same strain to William, and since then, the revelation of the wretched chit's true identity had not improved the case. "Perhaps not—but such an alliance would undoubtedly strengthen the bonds between the partners of the Bank," she suggested, ignoring the face that Christopher pulled at this remark. "And I believe Ebford would be bound to put Catherine's happiness before purely mercantile considerations. Don't forget, either, that if Melly can but secure the Colonel, then the Bank will have lost nothing but *we* shall have gained all!"

Christopher's head was now reeling. Good God, he thought desperately, *women!* How could one argue sensibly with them? 'Catherine's happiness', indeed! The sort of talk one might expect from a green girl, but pretty well from one such as his mother!

As for Ebford's real sentiments regarding his

adopted daughter, it was as plain as a pikestaff from the events of past weeks that the Bank's interests ranked higher with him than those of Catherine. And the Bank was indivisible from George Ebford himself, whatever fancies to the contrary might be indulged. His mother also seemed to be overlooking the trifling matter of Cathy's age: at only eighteen, Ebford's consent would have to be sought—unless Gretna Green also figured in her calculations.

There was an additional factor, too, which he did not like to mention to her. He was not privy to all the details, but knew enough to apprehend that all was not well these days between the two Partners. From the occasional hint here and there he had gleaned that his father had been making free with the Bank's funds in a style not likely to endear him to Ebford.

So he kept these latter reflections to himself, simply informing his theatrically disappointed mother that he could not be party to anything so daffish.

"Not even for that poor, dear girl's sake?" she persisted in a failing voice.

Goaded past endurance by this final sycophancy, he cried: "You drive me too far, ma'am, with your damned marplots! We shall all be under the hatches if you persist with them!" Whereupon he rose precipitately and left the room, his face, for once, as white as his father's.

NINE

At Challow itself Lucian was doing all in his power to set his guests at their ease, and to reconcile his sister with the lady of his choice. Partly with that in mind, upon their return from worship that first Sunday he had placed Catherine and the other two in Rosalind's hands to be shown around the house. For himself he pleaded urgent letters needing his attention, and did not appear again until dinner.

Miss Berrington took a fierce pride in Challow and, in the general way, was never happier than when extolling its qualities to visitors; that the house's future mistress was now among the latter she genuinely tried to forget for the present. Mrs Wilby was quickly enthralled by the unusual residence, and Catherine, freed of her host's agitating presence and conscious of his sister's better self-control, felt able to give all her attention to it. Even Melissa took a polite interest as, despite her previous visits, it was the first time she had seen over the entire building.

It proved easy for Miss Berrington to become less conscious that Miss Ebford was likely to usurp her position; for she had to concede that the young person displayed no tactless domestic interest in the establishment whatever, and nor did she thrust herself forward in other ways. In fact by the end of the tour, Rosalind, who was no fool, was fast coming to the conclusion that Lucian's enthusiasm for the match was by no means shared by his intended. She began to feel more hopeful and her manners improved still further: Miss Ebford, though in no respect an assertive girl, did not have the looks of one who would succumb against her will.

Lucian had not confided to her many details of his proposed marriage, but she had gathered that Lord Ebford and his precious Bank were to be the chief benefactors, and that her brother stood to gain little from that transaction. From that, it was a short step to convincing herself that he was the victim of a Machiavellian plot devised by Ebford to secure his accounts. Of course she was aware that her brother had an outstanding military reputation, and was even prepared to admit his talent as a man of affairs; but when it came to dealings with the opposite sex she would not allow him to know anything of the matter. No, an astute banker was quite clearly exploiting his infatuation with this girl, and that was all there was to it. She now had a shrewd notion that it might be vastly more profitable to broach the subject with her directly than risk brangling over it with Lucian again. Still smarting from his rebuke, she resolved to seize the first opportunity which offered itself for a private cose with Miss Ebford.

Catherine, unaware of her new-found ally, suffered a return of all her former apprehensions when the dread hour of dinner again approached. She was almost driven to confiding in her aunt that she intended to leave, but, knowing the futility of that course, spoke instead to Melissa when they had a few moments together in their room.

"I'm not surprised in the least!" ejaculated the latter. "Why, you were in such an obvious taking before church that I was perfectly sure you must have spurned the Colonel already, and were about to insist the carriage took us back to town!"

"If only I could have done. But how *am* I to get away from here, Melly? I know now that I have to...."

"Are you beyond all doubt that he is in love with you?" This was said with a certain spiteful incredulity which might have hurt her at any other time.

"Oh, yes," she sighed forlornly.

"But he has not precisely *spoken*, I collect?"

"There is no need for him to: I *know* from that look of his. It gave me the oddest sensation.... Observe him for yourself when we are together, if you don't believe me."

"Oh, I will, never fear!"

Catherine disliked the tone of this conversation, but persevered with it as, after all, Melissa was supposed to be here in order to help extricate her from this ever deeper entanglement. "You do see, don't you," she asked her earnestly, "that now there is not the smallest chance of deflecting his interest in your way?"

"Thank you! But I had already decided for myself that would not fadge," her friend said with dignity though looking decidedly miffed. "It was never more than a quiet nonsensical start of Mama's—and you were not one jot of help to it, coming down to dinner last night after all that we fixed!"

"I'm sorry, I just couldn't——" murmured Catherine. Every nerve of her was now on edge for the sound of the dressing bell.

Melissa's temper underwent another abrupt change. "Poor Cathy! You just couldn't carry it off, that was the case wasn't it? But don't fret! We'll find a way to smuggle you out, I daresay. I must say it's quite romantic and exciting, isn't it! But let me think. . . ." She placed a finger pensively on her dimpled chin, while her green eyes danced with mischief. "Yes!—Mr Frodsham, of course! He'd be up to any rig, I'll warrant!"

"No," said Catherine with severity. "He must not be involved—not in a scheme against his own uncle."

The plotter was a trifle dashed by this scrupulousness, but soon made an ingenious suggestion. "There's no call to tell him a thing! I shall merely propose we get up an expedition one day to the nearest town—just the three of us, and then you can take the chance to slip away."

"But it would never be permitted. Someone would be bound to accompany us. And besides, it would mean leaving you alone with Mr Moreton-Frodsham in a strange place."

But Catherine's punctilio on behalf of her friend was received with a complacent stare. "Pray don't put yourself out over a triviality of that sort! Now, do you want me to enlist the nephew's help or not?"

While Catherine hesitated and bit her lip, Acton's approaching firm tread was heard on the landing outside the chamber. "No, it cannot be right. . . . Oh, well, yes, I suppose so!" But she dared not contemplate what new hobble this might lead them into.

If Lucian had not held to his custom of inviting a half dozen of his neighbours to dinner on Sunday, he could scarcely have failed to notice that he came under the closest scrutiny from at least two pairs of female eyes that evening. As it was, his attention was fully absorbed ensuring that Catherine was made arm in armly with his great friends Lord and Lady Sylvern, and Squire Stokes and his family. Consequently, Rosalind and Melissa were both given a perfect opportunity to observe how he conducted himself towards Catherine. 'Besotted' was the word which sprang independently to the minds of both ladies, as each resolved to put a period to his infatuation in her own way.

Catherine, being by no means as oblivious of these cross-currents around the table as Lucian appeared to be, experienced the greatest difficulty in acting with any spontaneity, and felt as gauche as any schoolgirl with the strangers. However, Lady Sylvern and Mrs Stokes, with their charm and good sense, might have been chosen—as in fact they had been—to make her easy; and before the evening was out she found she was enjoying herself more than she had thought conceivable.

In the squire's lady, in particular, she was aware of a generous spirit coupled with great strength of understanding, and no affectation of manner whatsoever. Catherine looked upon Mary and Timothy, Mrs Stoke's children, of about her own age, with a bitter-sweet feeling that she knew to be envy: for to have a mother such as theirs was a dream she had cherished for as long as she could recall.

At one point in the drawing-room she had been seized with a desire to pour out her troubles to this benevolent lady; but the moment soon passed. The fact that she had not been blessed with a known parent gave her no licence to make proxy use of others', and so save her from relying upon herself, as she should do. She qualified this stern philosophy of self-reliance in relation to Christopher's help, which she had by no means yet despaired of, and, to a lesser degree, the assistance of Mr Moreton-Frodsham, who had now returned to the ladies in company with Timothy Stokes.

Felix, dutifully observing his uncle's wishes, proceeded straight to the side of Melissa, where his amiableness soon convinced her that she would easily be able to turn their acquaintance to good account when the time was ripe.

Mrs Wilby, who like Catherine had taken Mrs Stokes in particular liking, and who had judged her own two young charges very pretty behaved throughout, considered matters to be progressing very comfortably; a feeling that was shared by all present—with one notable exception—when the visitors took their leave.

"I do so hope that you found your neighbours—I mean, your new friends to your taste," Lucian said to her softly when they had gone.

This slight slip, so delicately and quickly rephrased, brought home to her once more the continuous impropriety of her position in this house. It also served to dispel all feeling of the genuine pleasure she had derived from the company.

"I have known the squire for ever, and his twins I find delightful—their likeness is most marked, is it not, for a boy and girl?" he continued smoothly when no immediate comment was forthcoming.

"Yes, indeed they are alike," she said slowly, conscious of her ill-manners but feeling that they hardly mattered in view of the much more Turkish treatment he would shortly have to endure at her hands.

"—And clipping riders, both of them, tho' perhaps you didn't touch upon that subject? All the talk seemed to be upon town topics, I fear."

"You do not care greatly for town life, I collect?" she murmured, more out of something to say than with any profound interest; but, to her dismay, this casual inquiry drew forth the fondest smile she had yet encountered.

"True! And I think I am guilty of having complained to you before how I dislike it—when I was actually *in* town: an unforgivable solecism! However, it was on that same occasion that I discovered your interest in riding, and so tomorrow—Ah, Rosalind." He broke off impatiently as his sister bore down upon them.

But Catherine, rendered speechless once more, was relieved to see his formidable relation. Her mind remained an obstinate blank as to the one or two short conversations she had engaged in with Mr Berrington before his Offer (presumably) was in his mind; it would have been strange were it otherwise, amidst the endless small talk of society; but he appeared to have remembered her every casual utterance. It made her overall feeling of *gêne* more insupportable still.

"I was just telling Miss Ebford that in the morning, if the weather allows, we shall all be making a grand circuit of the grounds. I trust you will make one of us?" he inquired with a certain edge.

"Of course I shall," Miss Berrington dourly confirmed. His coercion aside, she had not the slightest intention of having the pair of them remove themselves from under her eye until such time as she had determined a way of banishing Catherine from the house more permanently.

Catherine was now in the singular position of being both highly sensible of Rosalind's animosity while having to welcome it in the peculiar circumstances she was placed in. It occurred to her that she was now by no means alone in her desire to evade the marriage, for Christopher and Melissa were pledged to render her positive aid, there was Mr Frodsham, and very obviously Rosalind might well exceed everybody in zeal if she saw a chance of foiling the match.

With these more sanguine reflexions she faced the prospect of yet another day at Challow with reasonable equanimity. Even her situation could not wholly prevent her from looking forward to an opportunity for her favourite occupation—riding. At all events, she was not inclined to make excuses over it, and on the morrow she donned the blue habit which Mrs Wilby had so doggedly packed at the outset.

It was arranged that Miss Berrington was to drive Honora in the Dennet gig, and the rest of the party were to be mounted. When the time came Catherine and Melissa made their way to the stables in search of the animals which had been made ready for them.

The early sun slanted between the pillars of a long and colonnaded approach to stable buildings which matched the style of the house itself. "I am very sure, Cathy," Melissa told her, as they strolled along with the tails of their dresses caught over one arm and a whip in the other, "that you need not harbour the tiniest doubt that by the time this sun is gone down, Mr Frodsham will be my willing slave!"

The sublime, not to say preposterous confidence of this claim took her friend's breath away. "How can you say so?" she replied, without troubling to conceal her scepticism. Not that she would have denied Melly's quite stunning appearance now in her emerald green riding dress. This sported epaulettes, and was braided with gold down the front and halfway up the sleeves *à la militaire*. A muslin cravat, lace collar and ruffles at the wrist softened any masculine effect given by the tall-crowned and peaked hat, in the style of an officer's shako. But, as always, it was the unusual green eyes which dominated all else and held the attention: at the moment they had a decidedly wicked glint to them.

"Ah, I *know* it! But no matter if you don't believe me—I shall offer you positive proof before the week is out, when we whisk you off to Maidstone or wherever it is you wish to go."

But to her surprise, this generous offer was not greeted with any marked enthusiasm. "I should never have asked you," was Catherine's only response. She was perturbed at the thought of her hurling herself at the head of this barely known young man, solely to seek a favour for herself.

"Oh, pooh! *Il faut faire de necessité vertu*—as that gentleman himself might well express it!"

This phrase induced a silence between them, and by the time that Catherine had understood that it meant something on the lines of making a virtue of necessity (which did not seem entirely apposite) they were arrived at the arched gateway.

"I only hope I am not given Miss Berrington's horse, for she must ride twice as heavy as I," remarked Melissa with complacency as they entered the busy yard, and seeing the gig for that lady in the course of being prepared.

"Oh, hush!" Cathy giggled nervously. "Tho' it's true that she would make a doughty sight on the hunting field."

The question of mounts had not troubled her at all: she knew herself to be a capable horsewoman, and also felt confident that they would not be offered unsuitable beasts by their host; who, even she could not deny, had shown himself considerate in all things since they arrived.

At that precise moment he came out of one of the stables with his nephew to greet them. As the pair strode across the yard, and around the circular stone trough placed in the middle, she wondered how it was that she had been able to ignore Mr Berrington's London self so completely; for here he seemed to dominate any company the instant he appeared. The white-streaked hair, which had made him look old to her before, no longer seemed so. Indeed she fancied he looked younger each time she saw him. No doubt that owed to his Unfounded Hopes, she told herself sternly.

Mutual pleasure being expressed on all sides over the cloudless sky and the fine day it promised, Lucian told Felix: "Now, do you go off and introduce Miss Dauntry to her mount." He turned to Catherine with the smile that she was now ready for. "And if you will walk this way I will show you the fellow I have in mind for you."

Catherine followed him into the similarly well-built stalls contained within the stone façade. Each occupant boasted its name plate on the door, and after passing several such he stopped by an anonymous compartment housing, she supposed, a hired hack for her use.

"There!" he said, opening the gate. "I hope you shall become the greatest of friends—what say you to him, eh?"

She found herself the object of lively, intelligent-looking eyes. The horse was the prettiest bay she had ever seen. "Oh, he's perfect," she said simply; perfect in every way, for here was her opportunity at last to quit Challow unremarked. On the pretext of an early morning gallop, she could clearly put many miles behind her on this strong-coupled bay before any search was set in motion.

Misreading the shrewd appraisal in her face, Lucian observed: "I thought you'd take to each other, for you're both handsome to a fault: he, tho', is also as stout as steel," he added, almost as if endorsing her scheme. He handed her a bit of carrot from the depths of his riding-coat pocket.

As this was snatched daintily from her palm

she asked: "What's his name, Lucian?" Then her face burned. . . .

"The men call him Toast," he told her unconsciously. "But you may fix upon some other to your mutual satisfaction, if you so wish. Come, we'll take him out."

"Oh, I would not presume to change such a fitting appellation," she mumbled; gradually becoming aware that her discomforture came only in part from her slip with Mr Berrington's first name, but also from the circumstance that the gravel beneath her feet in the stall was a little awkward to stand upon. There was no straw in this stable; which intrigued her out of her embarrassment to the point of making her ask him about it.

"You are right, it's a trifle odd," he agreed as they stepped outside again with the bay. "It is by way of a small experiment I am conducting following a paper I read on modern equine care in one or two Continental countries. It seems to me the foreigners may well be right: *we* may find it mightily harsh stuff to stand on, but these creatures do seem to prefer it to a straw covering."

She could not help but be impressed by such careful thoroughness, and remarked as much, but he merely shrugged off the compliment and turned aside to call for a saddle. Whilst they were waiting he deliberately let drop one of his riding gloves; whereupon the horse at once retrieved it, returning it to him in exchange for a further titbit. He laughed. "There—it's well worth making such a polite fellow comfortable, is it not?"

She was just reflecting how extraordinary it was that a well-schooled horse of this stamp should be out for hire, when a stable lad ran up. "I hope you will not look askance at this old saddle," Lucian said, taking it for a moment from the boy, "but the new one is not due from the saddler until a day or so."

It was only then that her misgivings hardened that this was no hired hack. "You have had a special saddle made?" she questioned hesitantly.

He seemed surprised. "Why, of course! It was scarcely to be thought of that you would wish to tolerate this shabby affair for long."

"Mr Berrington," she said in a low voice so that the boy, now busy with the girth, should not overhear, "I cannot—you are not proposing to present me with—him?" she finished lamely, reaching to pat Toast's nose.

At this the straight brows lifted a fraction higher. "I have already done so, my dear girl! Now, if I may see you safely mounted you can join the others, and I will follow after."

Vexed at her slow-wittedness in not foreseeing that she might be the recipient of extravagant gifts in these circumstances, she allowed herself to be lifted into the saddle without demur. Then he stood back and, with a faint smile softening the natural scowl, said almost to himself: "Yes—the two of you make an even better picture than I had imagined." Louder, he added: "What of that footstall? Are you sure you are perfectly easy there?"

Indeed, at that moment she had never felt less so, as she contemplated the enormity of using his own gift-horse to enable her to run away, and doubtless cause him a good deal of distress; but, summoning up a smile, she reassured him and then turned all her attention to the essential business of getting on the best of terms with Toast.

The park around Challow had been laid out with military precision by General Sir John Berrington; and although the circuit boasted many of the features to be expected in larger grounds, they were linked in the main by perfectly straight avenues, sometimes enlivened by urns and statues set back in neatly clipped evergreen niches. Thus an impression was given of a temple of Flora huddled cheek by jowl with a pantheon, a palladian bridge with an obelisk, and a grotto with a fishing pavilion. All of these picturesque constructions had been deployed around an artificial lake which was itself very symmetrical and boasting a central island.

Under Rosalind's rigorous management the park had never lost the well-barbered look it had had from the first; a veritable army of scythers being needed in the summer months to maintain it. Lucian secretly looked forward to a time when he could impose a less formal aspect on his property, but for the sake of domestic peace this intention remained unvoiced. However, today he had overridden Rosalind's plans for refreshment to be taken in the small classic temple and had instead chosen a sheltered place beside the lake for an al fresco meal.

When he announced this altered scheme to the party, his sister glowered ominously from her driving seat in the gig next to Mrs Wilby, and for a moment it seemed almost as if she might refuse to stop by the waterside to allow her passenger to alight there. By then, however, the three younger riders had had more than their fill of making polite remarks on the museum-like edifices, and they dismounted with alacrity and thereby effectively checked the gig's further progress. Not that Melissa and Mr Moreton-Frodsham had taken a vast degree of interest in anything but each other this past half-hour, which had left Catherine as the only listener to some wry asides from Lucian upon the topic of his own dissatisfaction with his father's over-neat landscaping.

Herself favouring the current fashion for a more natural treatment in the design of gardens, she found she was in amused accord with most of his views; which only drew down more black looks on her from the sharp-eared Rosalind.

These pairings remained throughout the picnic, as no one seemed inclined to alter them. Following some half-hearted general conversation, the two older ladies soon had their heads together deploring the price of fresh vegetables, after Mrs Wilby had divulged to her hostess some scarcely credible intelligence that peas were risen to the prodigious price of six guineas a quart in town; and Melissa, true to her word, soon had her companion hanging ardently upon her every word.

Catherine's apprehension over the pair of them must have shown, for presently Lucian murmured to her: "There is not the smallest need to fret yourself over events in that quarter, you know."

As she had been wondering if Melissa could have possibly advanced so far with Mr Frodsham as to be broaching her own escape expedition, she was considerably startled by this observation. But she soon realized Lucian referred merely to the possibility of an unsuitable attachment forming between them, and with relief she denied any qualms on that head.

"For I have my own ways of restraining that young gentleman's transports," he continued, with a certain dour satisfaction which reminded her how old-fashioned and set in his ways he was.

Indeed she did not at all care for the conspiratorial role she had been cast in with Mr Berrington that day, and Toast or no Toast, she began to despair of ever contriving to avoid his affectionate but also excessively vigilant eye upon her.

They dined early at Challow (Monstrous Rusticism, in Melissa's declared opinion), and even when they retired to bed it was still scarcely dark. In addition, neither young lady was at all inclined to sleep, and they had thrown back the bed curtains; partly so that they would know if Mrs Wilby should enter through the communicating door.

As soon as their heads touched the pillows confidences flowed from Melissa. "Ahem—if Miss Ebford would caindly inform us at her leisure when she is desirous of leaving us, matters will, ahem, be set in train," she intoned in a voice tolerably like Miss Jamieson's, which mimicry usually amused them both.

But not on this occasion. Catherine sharply turned her head, causing the curl-papers to make their presence painfully known. "Melly—you haven't asked him *already?*"

"Pooh, I had no call to! But whenever you wish, it will be done. I *must* say, Cathy, I had quite thought you would go off into raptures," she went on crossly as the silence grew prolonged.

"Well, yes, I suppose that I am! But consider—now

that I'm at liberty to ride Toast, do you not think it might be preferable for me to slip away by myself?"

"No, chucklehead, I do not! Why, I'll warrant you don't even know which road to take from here for the nearest turnpike, do you?"

She waited impatiently throughout another glum pause before continuing: "Well, then! I declare you are the silliest creature, and without one drop of spirit in all your body! A perfect *natural* could see that if we escort you to the nearest stage office it will be *infinitely* more to the purpose!"

Crushed by these frank strictures, Catherine could only mumble: "And where is that, pray?"

"Oh, leave that to me, I shall discover everything from Felix, never fear. You see, I am teaching him French, and, as I foretold, he is my slave for life! It is fortunate beyond anything that he should dote upon the one foreign language that stupid Miss Jamieson managed to teach me! *And* it diverts him from reading his beastly boring poetry to me, too, which I have had to head off more than once already! So—should I wish to ask any awkward questions, concerning stage offices and the like, I can do so in French under the guise of instructing—isn't that quite *famous?*"

"Yes, famous," Catherine repeated dully. She wished more than ever that she had never sought Melissa's tempestuous helpfulness.

"Voilà! All that *you need* to do now is tell me where you want to go."

"But I don't know!" she cried.

"Don't know?—you *must* know, by now!"

"How can I? I am not acquainted with a single soul who might harbour me," she said with bitterness, at last abandoning all hope in Christopher. As she dismissed him from her mind, a tantalizing picture of Mrs Stokes's kindly features took his place; but she knew it was still not to be thought of to appeal to Mr Berrington's own friends. That his nephew was to be exploited was already the outside of enough. "Oh," she whispered with all her heart, "how I *wish* Ben were here!"

"Well, he isn't—and nor is that worthless brother of mine: wait till I get my hands on him."

Hope wavered back. "*Might* he still come? Perhaps I should wait. . . ."

"Not for that slow-top! If he should come, now, what odds that it will be *after* the announcement? Cathy, *do you still wish to be here then?*" she demanded with awful emphasis.

"Lord, of course not! But everything seems so vastly more difficult now I am here and not in town. Of course, I knew how it would be, that was why I strove so not to come."

"Listen, I think I have it!" Melissa had reared up excitedly on to one elbow. "Our cousin Henrietta! She lives here in Kent! Oh, she's a queer old thing, but quite a corky one in her day, according to family tales. *She* refused to wed merely to oblige her people, so I daresay she'll view your plight with some fellow-feeling—that's if she can still recall her own!"

Upon hearing this, real hope revived in Catherine's breast at last, and made her indifferent to the hurtful things which Melissa had said to her. "Oh, *thank you,* Melly! It sounds a perfect solution. If only I may stay with her for a week or two it will enable me to take stock of myself so as to embark on a new life." Her lips trembled perilously despite the brave words they had uttered, and she almost sobbed out: "I wonder why Christopher didn't mention her to me?"

There was a muffled snort as her friend sank back into the bed-clothes. "I told you—he's a slow-top!"

TEN

The air was hot and dusty in the clerks' office at Ebford's Bank. Charlie Bone sneaked a glance at the big clock on the wall, saw that it still lacked five minutes to eleven, and realized that only ten minutes had passed since his last furtive check. Sighing, he picked up his pen from the standish before him and dipped it once more in the ink; but before he could proceed with marking the ledger page he was diverted from this task by an irresistible vision which arose in his mind of a slice of currant pudding.

Eleven o'clock was invariably a bad time for Charlie, for he had a vocacious appetite, which was never more than partially assuaged by the meagre fare provided by his employer. The next portion of that was not due to him for many more hours, but in the meantime he had a thirty-minute break at mid-day when, on the days he had the means at his disposal, he could buy his own food. On such occasions his search for sustenance usually took him to the cheapest pudding shop in the Strand; where, however, they did not serve the rich and currant-strewn object of his present dreams.

He recalled that he had introduced Benjamin to the particular delights of the superior shop; where sometimes, and with the utmost generosity, his friend had bought him a fourpenny plate of beef. After Ben's sudden departure he had never had the beef again, and not solely because of its cost; he had felt it would not taste the same to eat it alone. He was a quiet boy who did not make friends easily, and so contrived to live a somewhat solitary existance while in the midst of numerous companions.

He forgot his hunger pangs momentarily, and fell to thinking about his lost friend and whether he would ever see him again. This he had pondered many times, but now it was quickened by a fresh anxiety. It had not escaped his notice that Ben's sister, Miss Ebford, did not visit the Bank these days. By dint of some cautious eavesdropping he had gleaned the news that she had gone into the country. His own belief was that she had been packed off there, but he couldn't have said why he thought so; unless it was the fact that the last time he had seen her quit the premises she was in pretty plain distress after being closeted with his lordship.

Charlie absently licked a finger and rubbed at a purple knuckle, then resumed his writing. A little more time crept past.

"Well, boys, is there no one to attend to the needs of Ebford's clients? It ain't much calculated to impress, and that's a fact!"

Startled by the unexpected voice, and more so by the abrupt manner of address, Charlie jerked his head up and beheld a large rubicund gentleman, whose head was as bare as if it had been tonsured, and who possessed the merriest and darkest pair of eyes, deepset in the face so that he was inevitably reminded of his phantom currant pudding again.

The stranger surveyed the room, which was empty of life save for two other clerks, even younger than Charlie, slumped in their high seats, and a dozen or so flies which hovered with equal lethargy overhead. He gave an expressive grunt, closing the door behind him and advancing further into the room.

"Sorry, sir!" Charlie piped up hastily, sliding off his well-polished perch. "Our Mr Rogers is the one as usually sees to things."

"No matter," said the visitor, holding up an expensively gloved hand and gripping a splendid beaver hat and silver-topped cane in the other. "I reckon you and I'll deal considerable well together, eh?"

"Yes, sir." Charlie had never heard anyone speak in this fashion before, but nonetheless there was something about the gentleman which made him take him in instant liking.

"Tell me, son, am I right to suppose the governor here is one Lord Ebford—Lord George Ebford?"

Charlie gave a vigorous nod. "That is to say, sir, Lord Ebford, yes! As to the George bit, I ain't quite sure. Not but what now you comes to mention it, I believe as it *is* George."

"First rate," the gentleman murmured. "Or I trust it may be!" he added, with a crack of laughter.

"Sir?" Charlie was becoming more and more confused. "I'll go seek out Mr Rogers, if you please."

But as he made to pass the stranger he was detained by a powerful arm. "No, I've a better notion. What's your name, boy?—well then, Charlie, I figure we'll leave your Mr Rogers out of this." He glanced at the other clerks, whose attention was riveted upon them, and bent down to whisper raspingly in the bewildered Charlie's ear: "Just tell me where I may locate his lordship and then forget you ever saw me, eh?"

But this suggestion was highly irregular to the experienced and conscientious clerk, and Charlie began to entertain a suspicion the pleasant-seeming visitor was in fact a rum cove. However, persuasive inducement was then offered him in the shape of a sixpence and an encouraging smile.

"Well—yes, sir," Charlie returned in a similarly low voice, and swallowing hard as the prospect of *three* two penn'orth slices of currant pudding floated before him. "That's if *you'll* forget you ever saw *me*."

The smile broadened. "You've got yourself a deal, boy. Now, we don't want to be caught together, do we?—oh, and here's a small consideration for your two friends' silence," he interposed with a wink over Charlie's shoulder. "So, if you'll oblige me with precise instructions of the governor's whereabouts, I will depart your humble servant."

Not without misgivings Charlie did as he was asked. Then he divided the largesse with the other pair, adding to that some suitably colourful injunctions for their discretion in the matter which concluded: "—or us may all be sent off with a flea in our ear and doomed to live on turn-round pudding, or worse, for the rest of our days!"

Elsewhere in the building their benefactor, having gained Lord Ebford's door without interception, hesitated there, ran a hand nervously over his bald pate, and then knocked with surprising timorousness for such a forceful-looking personage.

The voice that answered: "Enter!" was far from timorous. The well-dressed stranger braced himself, then opened the door.

"Mm?" said Lord Ebford, not lifting his eyes from perusal of a document on his desk as he presumed it was Rogers returned from his errand. "Well, speak, man, is the surety valid or not?" The prolonged silence induced him to look up at last. He ejaculated: "Good God!" Then, discerning quickly with his professional eye the intruder's prosperous air, his annoyance was modified a trifle. "And who might you be, sir?"

Two sets of what were in fact markedly similar eyes met each other; although his lordship's lacked the twinkling quality he beheld in the other's.

The intruder said slowly: "Do you know. I don't believe I'd have had to ask you that, George, even after all these years. But I, alas, am the more changed by time's winged chariot, as they say. Gone bald as a vulture, ain't I, *and* as fat as a flawn!"

The combination of an alien accent with the wholly unlooked-for familiarity brought Lord

Ebford to his feet and he glowered across the big desk. His hand groped for the silver bell upon it.

"No, I beg you . . ." the stranger said in a different tone altogether. "You and I do not require witnesses to this meeting, as I'm sure you will shortly agree." He paused, smiling uncertainly. "But should there be any, unbidden, then you may make me known as Robert Barton of Philadelphia."

"Robert?" the other uttered hoarsely. *"You!"* He reseated himself, looking stricken, and opening his mouth several times before saying: "You once gave me your word as a gentleman that you would never make any attempt to see me again after you left these shores."

"True," Mr Barton agreed with composure. "And the fact is, I didn't make any push to seek you out, but dammit!—I was just walking down the Strand and what do I espy but the name Ebford, writ large before me! You've got to see it was only human nature to discover if it were indeed my own brother."

The banker winced visibly. "I have no brother," he announced to the ceiling. "What do you want?"

"By golly, George, you do know how to make a fellow welcome! How do I know what I 'want' from you? As I just said, I didn't anticipate this meeting any more than you did. In a sense it's your own doing—after all, if you hadn't prospered and set up your business here for all the world to see, it just wouldn't have come about!"

"Would that I hadn't then," came the cold response.

"No, you can't mean that, George!" And Mr Barton wagged an admonishing finger. "Never denigrate success. You see before you the founder of *Barton's Bazaars*—famous, I may say, throughout the Union—and he is not complaining nohow!"

"That is a change, at least," his elder retorted dryly. He appeared unimpressed by these trans-Atlantic achievements. "If you don't care for my attitude towards you, permit me to refresh your memory, Robert. Fourteen years ago—in 1800, when it was 'a new century, a new country and a new name' for you, as I think you phrased it at the time—with your long-suffering wife finally deceased, you were—how shall I say?—somewhat *hard run,* and playing least in sight with your creditors. In short, you were at a stand."

Robert rested his hands on his cane and slightly hung his head before this trenchant, and, he had to admit, all too accurate obloquy. However, by confronting his brother he had invited censure, and, by golly, he sure was getting it! he reflected.

"In those deplorable circumstances I and my dear wife—she was taken from me not long after, by the bye—gave sanctuary to your offspring and funds to yourself, *on condition* that thenceforth you would be as one dead in England. I have abided by that to the letter: I wonder why you could not!"

"George," he began again patiently, "this is by way of the most minor transgression of what was then arranged. It became necessary for me to make a trip here for business purposes. The rest was sheerest chance, as I keep telling you: but even you could hardly expect a man to pass by such a chance once it offered." He paused, adding sadly: "I have often bethought me of the boy and girl, how else could it be?"

"Quite other, I would have surmised, judging by

the lack of concern you displayed for them when you were here."

Mr Barton drew himself up a little. "You have every right to castigate me, of course—but don't imagine I have not spent fourteen exiled years regretting my youthful follies."

"Youthful follies! Ha! You were gone thirty at the time."

"You are very severe upon me still, George," the younger man murmured, all of his earlier ebullience gone. "Am I to be told nothing of my children's subsequent life, then?"

The Banker took time to consider this home question: with Catherine set to wed Berrington, who had been told of her true origins but that both her parents were long dead, it would be crass folly to place the match in jeopardy by the sudden resurrection of the disreputable rogue before him; who would doubtless be returning to his American bazaars soon enough. As to Benjamin, it still pained him deeply to dwell on his ingratitude. Like father like son, he reflected, and would have enjoyed hurling that particular shaft at Robert. But that was a luxury he could ill afford, he decided; he did not desire any prying into his affairs by this feckless relative.

Although he would not have admitted it to himself, much of his rancour stemmed from the fact that Robert had fathered a perfectly sound son whom he had abandoned; while his own much-cosseted boy was more than a little mad. "No: it would serve no useful purpose for you to know anything of your children," he said at last.

"I do not ask to see them—but you must surely apprehend my interest in their welfare?"

"Forgive me, Robert, if I find this somewhat belated attentiveness a shade repellent. The answer is still, no. You have seen me, much against my will, and that must suffice."

Not yet entirely crushed, Mr Barton mopped his shining head with a large handkerchief and persisted with determined formality: "I should like, before I go, to express my gratitude for all you have done over the years. And, as I'm fairly swimming in lard these days, would you permit me at least the privilege of franking my—the children from here on? The girl must now have reached marriageable age, and a good solid dowry would——"

"No!" the other shouted, standing. "I'll hear no more from a dead man! You will oblige me by leaving at once before my chief clerk returns. I dare swear you can find your own way, since you inveigled yourself in!"

He was well accustomed to repulsing a supplicant; though never before with such violence. Mr Barton shrugged and went, leaving behind him not only an angry kinsman but also an excessively troubled one.

ELEVEN

Lord Ebford had every cause for disquiet; he now bitterly repented having divulged Catherine's parentage to Lady Olivia, after having kept it secret for so many years. It seemed almost as though Robert had been conjured out of the air in response to a mere mention of his existence. The wretched fellow's visit had left him stunned. When this feeling dissipated, he was doubly impatient to receive Berrington's tidings of the official betrothal, although he knew it to be the purest formality. But now he trusted in nothing going right: he even wondered whether to drive into Kent posthaste, before receiving any summons; but that would give a devilish odd appearance and, superstition aside, there was no logical reason to suppose his brother would pursue the matter further after meeting with such a monumental rebuff.

Even if he did wish to—how could he conceivably set about it? His lordship felt a trifle more reassured.

Mr Robert Barton was pondering that very problem; but a sense of helplessness was very absent from his approach to it. He had not created his small empire of *Barton's Bazaars* by backing off from the first trifling setback put in his way. *No, sir!* he thought, as he stared unseeingly at a printmaker's window about fifty yards from the entrance to the Bank.

As he moved gradually and unwillingly away along the street, a tantalizing whiff of roast beef assailed his nostrils and made him mindful of the fact that he was very hungry; and, as he always thought better on a full belly, he turned his nose here and there like a hound-dog, endeavouring to track down the aroma to its source. But this procedure soon led him to the opening of a rather mean and unenticing alleyway. He sighed, and was about to turn back and seek out a more high-class establishment when he descried a thin and faintly familiar figure, clad in rusty black and studying the bill of fare pinned outside a humble eating-house. He walked decisively down the alley, calling: "Charlie!—well met once more, eh?"

Young Mr Bone, freed from the constraints of the office and wrestling with the taxing problem of how best to dispose of his sixpence, gave a nervous start, at once prey to fears that the latter was in danger of being snatched back from him. "Sir?" he said with more apprehension than pleasure in his tone, and holding tightly on to the coin.

But the stranger's descending hand merely

landed heartily between his scrawny shoulders. "I would deem it a considerable privilege, my boy, if you'll take a bite to eat along with myself." He lowered his voice confidentially. "Somewhere where we may be private and unobserved by your fellows at the Bank, if you understand me?"

Mr Bone did, very well: few gentlemen of any standing desired to be seen with an impoverished clerk; although why this one should wish for his company at all eluded him. "Well, sir, the best dining-room in this place is sort of sliced into compartments with tall-backed seats, like."

Mr Barton beamed. "Fine! Shall we repair there?—and you're sure your companions won't be encountered within?"

"Lord, no! It's way above their touch, sir! When you come along I was only just thinking of a fourpenny plate of beef to eat outside," he confessed with disarming frankness.

"Well, then," said his twice benefactor, pushing open the door and thereby setting several little bells into tinkling motion, "you may save that for another day."

As Charlie followed him in he was suddenly assailed by his former doubts about the gentleman being a rogue of some kind. He wondered if he'd been a fool to succumb to such an offer on the one day when he was able to buy himself a dinner fit for a king; but then that, too, was due to the stranger's generosity. It was all very disturbing. . . .

After a murmured exchange with Mr Barton, and a surreptitious transfer of coins, the waiter showed them to the darkest alcove in the depths of the best dining-room; which seemed dingy enough for any fell purpose after the sunlight outside. . . .

"Sir," Charlie stuttered out, just as soon as he had seated himself, "pray don't get thinking that I'm not fully conscious of the honour you do me, but I hope you will not reckon it impertinent of me to inquire why—that is—for what purpose——?" Dismissal from the Bank now beginning to loom large in his imagination, he floundered in a sea of unaccustomed verbiage.

"Take it easy, Mr Bone! You shan't wind up in Newgate or the colonies on my account—that's as long as you ain't a tonguey lad, and I don't think you are."

"Tonguey?" the clerk repeated blankly.

"You'll have to forgive me: I've lived in America for many years and have picked up a somewhat motley vocabulary on the way. Talkative, was what I meant to say. I must know if I can depend upon you to keep this meeting, and anything we may discuss, strictly to yourself."

"Well—yes, sir. But as I'm not even acquainted with your name, it's not as if I'd be able to reveal very much, like." He paused, hoping that this cunning riposte would extract that much information at least before he had to commit himself.

"Ah, but it might be enough! Just a description of me in the wrong quarter could suffice to do a deal of harm, boy."

Before Charlie had the opportunity to inquire as to what the 'wrong quarter' might be (and he fervently hoped that it wasn't the Runners) his companion was saying: "So, I have your word? Come, you may trust me, I do assure you." Seeing the hesitation still lingered on the clerk's face, he added: "My purpose is in no way nefarious, I swear: I merely seek a little information about two young people."

The waiter intervened at that crucial point, bearing two steaming, mountainous plates, and set them down before the clerk's awed eyes. Barton smiled with a kind of tactful pity as he regarded him from the opposite bench in the alcove. "I took the liberty of ordering when we came in, Charlie, as I guessed you may be short for time. I trust it meets with your approval?"

A grin of delight answered him succinctly. "Mutton and smash! Oh, yes, sir! You think of everything—'cause I do only have a half-hour at my disposal, like." And indeed, he took up his knife and fork as if it were but half a minute.

"I figured as much: yes, George would be a regular driver." But luckily his youthful companion was now far too engrossed to notice this slight familiar lapse. "Well now, to business! If, between mouthfuls, you could answer me this I shall stand forever in your debt: do you know ought of Lord Ebford's family?"

He could not express himself more precisely, as he had no idea if George had claimed Ben and Cathy as his own or merely as step-children; nor in fact did he know what family he had of his own, apart from vaguely recalling a rather odd, silent little fellow a shade older than Catherine.

The mention of his esteemed employer had done little to benefit Mr Bone's digestion. At once he ceased chewing, and began to choke slightly upon what was then in his mouth. "Very little, sir," he said after swallowing hastily. "That is, beyond seeing Miss Ebford come in the Bank now and then." That was common knowledge, so must be tolerably safe to tell, he assured himself.

"You mean Miss *Catherine* Ebford?" Barton's own food remained untouched.

Charlie stared back at him. "Why do you ask questions about her?" he demanded with sudden sternness, remembering his suspicions that *she* might have disappeared now, as well as Ben. Could this cove know something about his friend?

"My interest is a wholly benevolent one, I promise you."

Charlie's pale blue eyes continued to scrutinize his companion's face, but after a moment he began eating again. He had decided to trust him for the time being, though without being at all sure why. But after all, it wasn't as if he had a great deal to disclose. He told him: "Mr Benjamin I knew pretty well, better than his sister, like."

Barton had all at once jerked upright, making the crockery dance. He leaned forward, pressing clenched fists against the wood. *"Knew?* Dear God—he's not dead, is he?"

This impassioned response did more to endear him to Charlie than anything he had said hitherto. "No, sir! At least, I hope not! You see, sir, the way of it was, he was put to the Bank to work, but after only two weeks he left—ran away, it was said—that was about a year ago, now."

Barton rushed further questions at him; to which he replied only guardedly, determined not to reveal the part he had played in handing over Ben's letter to his sister.

"And has *nothing* been done to discover his present location?" The stranger now sounded very wrathful, and his colour had deepened alarmingly.

"I don't believe so, sir," Charlie faltered. He suddenly decided to take the risk of unburdening his anxieties concerning Miss Catherine to this clearly most concerned audience.

"The girl's *banished,* you say? Good God, the man's a monster! I always knew it!" Small wonder, then, that George had greeted him with less than enthusiasm if both the children were missing. . . . He found it hard to believe nonetheless, and, taking a draught of restorative ale, suggested reasonably: "But couldn't she have gone into the country to stay with friends, perhaps?"

"Oh, she could that," Charlie had to agree. "But the town's not empty of the Quality until next month in the ordinary way, and this year there are all manner of kick-ups extra to do with the celebrations, as you must know, sir. Besides, though I daresay this ain't to the point, I did think as Miss Ebford looked a trifle unhappy the last time I saw her at the Bank, like."

Mr Barton, not unnaturally, thereupon posed innumerable questions to his informant regarding his long-lost offspring, but Charlie, becoming increasingly conscious of the passing time and as to where this encounter might be leading him, soon said he would have to leave.

"Yes, of course—and we haven't resolved matters yet, have we: now consider this very carefully, Charlie, if you will. Do you know of anyone who might lend a sympathetic and, above all, a discreet ear to my inquiries about our two young friends?"

The boy's lean features were quite contorted by

the effects of his deep deliberations combined with the anxiety to be back safely amongst his ledgers. "There is *one* gentleman," he murmured finally. "Mr Christopher—Dauntry, that is." He went on to explain the latter's standing at the Bank, adding: "I ain't in the know, of course, but I sort of thought Miss Catherine and he might marry one day."

Mr Barton pounced eagerly on this nugget. "And so it could be that she has been sent out of this fellow's way, mayhap?"

"I don't know nothing about that, sir." Although now he thought on it, young Mr Christopher had seemed sort of desponding of late; he wondered if his inquisitor might not have hit the nail on the head.

"Well, just remember that your confidences are quite secure with me. And if you do have any more thoughts on this delicate matter which you feel might help, a message to Mr Barton at the Clarendon, Bond Street, will find me. Now, before you cut along, may I have Mr Dauntry's direction?"

Charlie satisfied this last request and thankfully scuttled away to the Bank; where that afternoon he and his two fellow clerks, all replete on Mr Barton's bribes, distinguished themselves by falling asleep to a man.

Their provider experienced a far more strenuous afternoon. Upon leaving the chop-house he returned straightway to his hotel, donned his most imposing raiment, and then hailed a passing jarvey to convey him to Portland Street.

His luck was in: Christopher who had not been into the Bank that day, was on the point of quitting the house when the butler opened the door to the visitor. Upon learning that it was himself the ruddy-faced individual was wishful of seeing, Chris examined the proffered card. '*Mr Robert Barton of Phil. U.S.A.—proprietor of Barton's Bazaars*' was inscribed in florid type. He frowned in puzzlement. "Sir, are you in any doubt you have the right person? If it should be a banking matter, then my father is your man, not I."

"No, sir: *you* are my man—and I crave a word in private on a question of some urgency which may touch upon both our interests."

This earnest address had its effect upon Christopher, and he decided that it could do no harm to talk to the fellow. Intrigued, he led him to the morning-parlour, the only sanctuary available to them; his father's study was out of bounds for him, and he did not fancy contending with his mother's birds in the drawing-room; or, for that matter, with her own possible intrusion.

"You are an American, I collect?" he asked, closing the door behind them.

"No: but I've been over for a good many years, and can claim to have made my way there tolerably well."

Christopher was relieved at least not to be entertaining an enemy; a consciousness which made him say next: "You must have crossed the Atlantic quite recently, then. Was that not monstrously hazardous, with the war still in progress?"

Robert Barton settled himself in the chair drawn up for him by the young man, whose demeanour he was studying closely from behind his bluff smile. It was now being borne in upon him that he might possibly be looking at his future son-in-law, if Mr Bone's surmise was accurate. He grunted:

"Lordy!—an ocean crossing would *always* make me quake pretty considerable, sir!—war or no war. And had I been able to choose I'd as lief have embarked on a Yankee ship and not a British—tho' I dare swear you'll dub that traitorous talk! As it was, I had to tell my captain all the way across what fine fellows they were, to keep our spirits up!"

Christopher, who had paid little enough heed to the war with America since its commencement two years before, had forgotten it completely since the overthrow of Napoleon, which had overshadowed everything else in Politicks. "You consider the Americans superior to our own folk?" he asked a shade stiffly.

"Aye, I do," Barton answered him squarely. "Certainly at sea, and very like on land as well. But I did not come here and impose on you just in order to air my contentious views on the war."

His face gave little away; but in fact he had been favourably impressed by both his young host and the very elegant style of this house. He made up his mind to proceed without more delay to the object of his visit. "Mr Dauntry, I believe you are acquainted with a Miss Ebford, is that correct?"

Christopher was so dumbfounded by this abrupt turn to the conversation that he could only nod in his solemn fashion; instead of asking what dashed business it was of his, as no doubt he should.

"Ah! Does that mean you are privy to her present whereabouts?" Another nod, albeit a scandalized and almost imperceptible one, was vouchsafed him. "Fine!" he continued with untrammelled ebullience. "And now, if you will permit just one further question, which is of a personal nature—but not asked in any idle spirit, I promise you: does any attachment exist between you?"

To that point Christopher had lacked assurance as to how best to deal with this queer character, but now he was in no doubt whatsoever. He came to his feet, observing in gelid accents: "You go beyond the line of what is pleasing, sir—who the devil are you?"

Mr Barton, quite unflustered and taking account of the young man's roseate hue, reached the conclusion that the answer to his question was indubitably yes. "You must forgive me, Mr Dauntry,' he said, also rising. "Indeed you have every cause to feel outrage—but my own position is awkward in the extreme, and I must perforce take a certain calculated risk in all this. I had to be sure you were the right person to share my little secret. I believe you are—and so if you will only bear with me a while longer I'll do my best to enlighten you."

With reluctance Christopher complied, and both gentlemen resumed their seats. "Jupiter!" he breathed, when the tale was finished. "So you're not a Barton but an *Ebford!*" He studied the robust features before him for any hint of a likeness to Catherine; soon giving up. Perhaps there was a slight resemblance to Benjamin, though even there——"Forgive me, but can you offer proof you are Catherine's father?"

"I don't believe I can, you know," was the candid response. "George will deny it till he turns up his toes—and understandably, since I'm supposed to have turned up mine many years back! Besides, I didn't come here to raise a rumpus—no sir! I just had this urge to come home before it was too late—this damnable war, you know. I never planned on seeking out my folks." He leaned forward confidentially. "Now, I'm not one to lay claim to having premonitions, like the ladies might, but *damme,* when I learned that Ben has vanished —and about the very same time I took this notion into my head—well, I *wonder* sir, *damme* if I don't!"

Christopher had to make a rapid decision whether or not he believed this Banbury story. Finally, like Charlie Bone before him, he did feel he could place a degree of trust in Mr Barton. However, he was influenced in that decision by another consideration which occurred to him: Catherine's father (if it were indeed he) seemed heaven-sent to help him extricate her from her impending marriage. Indeed, Mr Barton had arrived when he himself had been on the point of finally ordering the chaise to carry him into Kent on the morrow. For ever since his mother had demanded his direct intervention, and he had refused, he had been in a state of perpetual indecision. After what he had been told that was now over: he was resolved to do what he could, whatever anyone might think of him.

He lost no time in putting his own sorry account before Mr Barton; and was then faced with the no small difficulty of restraining the frantic parent from setting forth for Kent there and then.

"Dastardly!—Infamous!" he had kept alternating throughout, and now he was upright again with further impassioned demands for immediate action.

"Hold hard, sir! I have every intention myself of posting there in the morning." He paused, unwilling to reveal either Berrington's name or whereabouts in case this fellow should still prove an impostor.

Mr Barton glowered at this lack of lover-like ardour, as he saw it. "Tomorrow may well be too late," he pronounced in a voice laden with doom.

"Come, now—we can hardly act before then, the day is far advanced already."

The other gave a reluctant murmur of agreement. "Yes, you're in the right of it: me, I'm too damned impetuous—always have been, or I'd never have given up those two little defenceless mites in the first place. But I'll make up for it now, by God I will! I'll discover Catherine first, and then my poor Ben—tho' where I begin on *that* quest, the Lord only knows!" His eyes were bright with unshed tears.

It was then fixed between them that Christopher should take him up at the Clarendon early the next morning. This arranged, he himself saw the unexpected caller quietly to the door, so that his mother might perhaps be fended off if she came into the hall. But she did not, and he breathed a great sigh of relief as he closed the panel behind Mr Barton's bulky form, for he knew that his powers of deception in that quarter were not strong.

TWELVE

After five days of suffering the presence of her brother's Choice, Miss Berrington was still awaiting an opportunity to take Miss Ebford to one side, and broach the very vexed question of her plighted troth before Lucian could attend to it himself.

That it *was* a vexed question Rosalind was now left in no doubt; throughout the whole of the chit's time with them thus far, she had observed her well-bred but really quite evident indifference to her brother. Indeed, if he had not been so *languishing* all the time he could not have remained insensible of it, she thought with renewed exasperation. But he seemed to her to be as one in a dream, and she could not suppose that it was likely he would brook much further delay before making a formal announcement.

They were all promised to the Stokes's at the manor later in the day, but not long after breakfast Miss Berrington, who kept the two young ladies under fairly constant surveillance, saw them hesitating on the gravel drive below the main steps. She continued with her unabashed vigil by the window until they appeared to fix upon a destination and turn off towards the orangery, then she hastened for her own bonnet and shawl: reasoning that it was better that she should speak to the girl outside the house, if that could be contrived, and confident that a word to the other pretty miss that Felix was on the look for her would soon ensure her speedy departure. With a grim smile of resolution, she mounted the stairs with a remarkable alacrity for one verging on the stout.

In the garden it was already warmer than inside the mausoleum-like house, and Catherine and Melissa proceeded at a strolling pace across the dewy lawn.

They were not talkative; Melissa by this time having tired of her role of conspirator, though not of the concomitant task of instructing Felix in French; and Catherine was simply becoming more and more dismayed as to her future with every deceitful day that passed here. Although, had it not been for that dreadful uncertainty which filled and blighted her every moment, she was wistfully conscious that she would have enjoyed her time at Challow. But as it was, she despaired of ever being carefree enough again to take pleasure in such frivolities. On the contrary, after her proposed brief stay with the Dauntrys' Cousin Henrietta, it seemed inevitable that she must straightway seek out gainful employment of some nature, and without further delay. Whether the eccentric cousin would be eccentric enough to lend any assistance in forwarding that scheme, seemed highly unlikely; for ladylike rebelliousness had not taken that form in her day. All that she could do in the meantime was occasionally count the guineas hidden away in one of her reticules, and wonder how long she could hope to survive on them.

"Oh, Cathy, do we *have* to go as far as the wretched orangery?" Melissa complained. In fact she viewed walking, at any time of the day, as a tiresome exertion devoid of reward, unless Mr Moreton-Frodsham might espy and join them. This had not transpired, and so she was a little out of patience, saying impatiently: "We're well enough away from the house here, and there's not a soul to listen to what we tell each other."

Catherine tilted her parasol and looked doubtfully about her; by now, she suspected every bush and shrub at Challow of over-hearing what was in—or, rather not in—her heart. "I think there is a sort of sunken garden which leads off this avenue, over there by the yews. That will serve better, I daresay." Despite this excess of caution, she was all impatience to hear her friend's news.

Sure enough, there was an opening in the high and immaculately-cut hedge, and they stepped through it into an enclosed garden. This consisted of more close-clipped hedging, but none growing more than a foot high and planted in a maze-like geometric pattern.

"I vow I've not set eyes upon one decent-looking flower since we came here," Melissa opined, eyeing the late General's masterpiece of miniature topiary with crushing disfavour. "I refuse absolutely to venture another step through that apology of a parterre—let's sit here in the shade, for now it is growing beastly hot, as well as wet!"

Brushing aside a few dead leaves, which had somehow escaped the attentions of those fanatical gardeners who would maintain the surroundings, they sat down on a stone bench which was set back in an alcove sculpted from the thick avenue hedge. There, as they drew closely together, Melissa's information was at last disclosed.

"Well, it is fixed that Felix will drive us to Maidstone tomorrow: just the two of us, no poor, dear Mrs Wilby."

Catherine felt her future closing in upon her, as inexorably as a trap upon a poacher; quite forgetting, for a moment, that this course was supposed to represent an escape for her. "Tomorrow!" she repeated, unable to keep a hint of dismay from her voice. "But, pray, what have you told him?"

"Only that you wish to undertake some private shopping commissions—in particular a present for La Wilby. Was not that most *devious* of me, Cathy?"

"He doesn't keep his own carriage, surely?"

"No, of course not—he will bespeak one from his uncle."

"Then it won't be allowed! And, in any event, Mr Berrington might then squire us himself!"

"You goose, why ever should he, for a boring female shopping expedition, don't you know *anything* of gentlemen's likes?"

"I know I cannot like this," Catherine said flatly. "And how can I be assured that Maidstone is the right place for my purpose? Does a coach run from there to Bromley?"

"Yes, yes, yes, to all your ditherings! I have wormed so much out of Felix, on the boring subject of Maidstone, that I could positively scream—all in French, too! My brain is splitting with that curst tongue! But, lucky for you if not me, Felix knows the town well enough. It seems there is but a single inn of any pretension, which I will conduct you to as soon as we arrive."

"Mr Frodsham will have to apprehend in due course that I'm not returning here—what if he raises a hue-and-cry?"

A heavy sigh greeted this last question, followed by the irascible words: "Catherine—do you or do you not want to leave here before Berrington proposes?"

"You *know* I do, save for——"

"Then I wish you will not be forever throwing rubs in the way of everything that is done for you! All that need concern you is that you reach my cousin's roof."

"If she is at home."

"There you go again!" Melissa ejaculated, her green eyes flashing dangerously. "Old Henrietta never travels abroad, in truth she scarcely sets foot outside the door, which in some part comprises her oddity, you see."

"Oh." And even Catherine, in her highly perturbed condition, perceived that this was not the moment to inquire into the other parts. "Perhaps you had best tell me her direction now, and I'll commit it to memory." She would much have preferred that a note be sent ahead of her intimating the fact if not the sorry detail of her arrival;

but had to allow that that would be hard and hazardous to contrive. Nonetheless she determined at least to request Melly to pen a billet which she could bear with her, and thus preserve a modicum of countenance when first meeting the eccentric Henrietta.

"Oh, very well, if it will make you feel better! And she is Miss Oaks of Swan Moat, and very well known in the district," Melissa told her.

Rosalind Berrington, who for the past several minutes had taken root in the avenue leading to the orangery, made haste back to the house after learning Miss Ebford's precise destination. Her step was springy, and her spirits had lightened considerably since she came outside. Thick-skinned though she was, she felt relief to have been spared the kind of direct clash with Catherine which she had thought unavoidable until this point. But now, to have overheard the whole of this girlish escapade seemed to her beyond everything propitious.

Her first instinct was to carry it to her brother, and have the satisfaction of saying, *I told you so*. But she curbed this desire: he would know soon enough, and more instructively. However, if the subject of the expedition to Maidstone should be aired in her official hearing, she would not be slow to give it her fervent blessing. So, to ensure that Mrs Wilby would not jeopardize the chit's flight by her untimely chaperonage, she resolved to seek out that lady with a kind invitation to accompany her next day on some morning visits.

She was just quitting the library, leaving behind a startled but highly flattered Honora, when Machin paced across the floor to tell her that

Lucian had been asking for her. Giving a cluck of annoyance, she proceeded towards his study. However, by the time she greeted him she had recalled her little secret, and, for once, felt in perfect charity with him.

Her rare look of good humour did not escape her brother, and he ruefully reflected that the next few minutes would soon banish it. He endeavoured to broach his subject in as lenient a fashion as he could, but it was not easy.

"Ros, I know it is your wish to be apprised of my plans betimes, so that the household shall not be shaken up unduly. So—I must tell you that it is my intention to ask Lord Ebford down for next Friday, and on the day following there will be a formal gathering here to mark the occasion of my betrothal."

He watched the bold eyes for an inevitable storming at that point, but it did not come. Instead, he almost had the impression that they softened towards him.

"By all means," she said impassively, and then appeared to transfer her attention to the walnut bureau. With her height, she had no difficulty in running a finger round the edge of the carved top. "Really!" she exclaimed, looking askance at the small harvest of dust she had gathered. "The new maid is neglectful of the bellows—I must speak with Carter."

"There's no call for that. I told the girl myself that she need not put herself out over this room. You know I had rather suffer a peck of dust than find my papers blown all over the floor." He said this with good-natured restraint, and also a certain resignation, knowing only too well that she did not care for anything which she could regard as interference in her domestic regimen.

Her brows drew together in a frown. "Pray don't confuse the servants Lucian."

"She was *not* confused—relieved, perhaps, after having seen the hugger-mugger in here."

He smiled, anxious to restore the rare amicability which had prevailed between them before this digression. "Then I may depend upon you for next week's arrangements? As to numbers, I will let you know as soon as replies are to hand from these invitations." He indicated the pile of gilt-edged cards reposing on his desk.

She cast them a neutral glance; but was then shocked and affrighted to see the printed coupling of his name with Miss Ebford's. A tremor ran through her, and she replied unsteadily: "You may depend on *me,* but I should not place over-much dependence in—in that quarter." She gestured blindly at the cards, unable to resist the temptation to speak out against such naïve and foolish confidence.

His steady grey eyes met her defiant ones. "You have left me in no doubt you don't care for my choice of bride——" he began patiently.

"No!—and no more does she!" came her further unguarded response.

He paled. "You had best explain that remark," he said levelly.

She was by this time in such a state of high dudgeon that she did so, scarcely aware of what she was saying as she retailed the girls' talk.

The lines on his face were like deep cuts by the time her tale-bearing was done. He grated out: "If it proves you are mischief-making—I'll show you no mercy. You will leave this house forthwith."

He had taken it even harder than she had imagined, and her anger now fought with pity. She was relieved to be able to swear that she had recounted nothing that was not true.

His harsh stare lingered upon her a moment more, and he seemed about to say something else to her, but finally shrugged and looked away. The taut silence between them lengthened until she felt she could bear it no longer, saying in a rush of words: "I collect the arrangements for next week are to be cancelled?" Her usual strident tones were tempered, and free of all trace of gloating.

He gave a queer little smile. "No, let them stand."

Taken aback, she drew a sharp breath to reply; but for once thought better of it, and left him, her expression gradually resuming its habitual dour cast. Oh, what an unmitigated fool she had been to warn him, she fumed to herself. *Of course* it was now the easiest thing in the world for him to put a period to the young people's outing the next day. Indeed, she told herself savagely, instead of foiling the match she had most probably been instrumental in having it brought forward! She ran to her own room, there abandoning herself to racking sobs of hopeless frustration.

Whilst she was thus occupied Lucian did nothing so dramatic, but just sank wearily into a chair and rubbed his eyes, as if afflicted with a sudden incapacitating headache. As soon as Felix came in and saw him there, that perceptive young gentleman gave an uncomfortable cough and murmured with his customary heavy accent: *"Pardon,* Uncle. Not feeling the thing, eh? I'll look in later."

"Don't go," Lucian muttered, rousing himself with an effort. "Does your French prosper under— warm instruction?"

His nephew promptly flushed to the roots of his golden hair. "Yes, dashed fortunate! Miss Dauntry is most fluent, sir."

"Aye, fluent, just so: but you mistake if you think she's not a scheming little devil besides."

Felix's embarrassment increased; he doubted whether this exchange was conducive to his gaining possession of his relation's carriage next day for the purpose of escorting the said scheming devil on what, he suspicioned, might be an irregular expedition. However, he would broach the matter as he had promised Melissa. "Yes, sir," he agreed soothingly, "I dare swear that she is. Er, I—that is to say, we, Miss Dauntry and Miss Ebford and myself—would be greatly obliged if we might take the barouche to Maidstone tomorrow. When I say *take,* it don't signify I presume to drive it myself, of course, so it would mean using the coachman——"

His request faltered to a halt as he encountered a thunderous scowl from his relative. It occurred to him that Uncle Lucian—like so many other rich nabobs one heard mention of—begrudged a fellow the smallest thing he asked for; such as, in this instance, the use of an old and deucedly unfashionable carriage. If that didn't beat the Dutch for sheer miserliness, he would like to know what did!

His indignation took a more sober turn: God, in all likelihood, this sour phiz he wore betokened not merely a check to Melissa's design, but, far more importantly, the end of his own well-breeched trip to Paris likewise. *Drat all females!* he fumed inwardly. "I *told* them it wouldn't fadge!" he blurted out loud.

"Oh, have I said so?" Lucian returned, in oddly mild accents considering his black looks.

"Well, no, you ain't." Felix's mind revolved swiftly inside his head. "But y'know, to tell you the truth, Uncle, there could be something dashed smoky afoot!" To save his Paris visit, he was now coolly prepared to stoop to treachery. "Miss Dauntry pitched some Canterbury story about Miss Ebford being mindful to purchase a gift for her aunt— which contrives there should be *no chaperon with us.*" He paused, to allow the full import of this revelation to sink in.

"It sounds a perfectly credible intention to me." So it appeared that Rosalind had not lied, even in the smallest detail, he thought bitterly. "What did you suppose was the reason?—are you fearful that you might be abducted by Miss Melissa?"

"Dash it, no!" Felix protested, with more forcefulness than was due. "But the thing is, y'see, she's been asking me some devilish odd questions of late all about Maidstone, the inns there, and coach routes, and Lord knows what else about the damned place—all in French, too," he added disgustedly.

"Merely enlarging your vocabulary in an imaginative fashion, my boy," Lucian said straightfaced. "You refine overmuch on trifles, Felix! You may take the barouche and Simon-coachman with my blessing."

Felix stared, his jaw gone slack. "Truly, sir?"

He had never anticipated this outcome, and had approached his uncle merely to humour Melissa's queer start. After the stern sermon Lucian had given him at the very first concerning the Ebford girl, he had never thought to have her entrusted to his care for a whole day virtually unchaperoned.

"Truly. And now you must forgive me, but there are so many pressing matters requiring my attention." He gestured vaguely at his desk; then looked away from it, stricken afresh.

Felix fixed his own eyes upon the large heap of invitation cards, interpreting the sight of it rather differently. "By the bye, sir, you'll say, won't you, when it's time for me to cut stick? Don't need to tell you—wouldn't wish to outstay my welcome."

"Never fear, I shall," Lucian told him with the faintest of smiles. "Now, sherry off, my dear fellow, if you will. Write an ode, or conjugate some French verbs! Oh, and Felix—don't think I am not obliged to you for your selfless vigilance where my guests are concerned."

Felix grinned uncertainly, finding his uncle's mood a shade unpredictable. He left him with a deep and flowing brow which would have passed muster at the court of Louis the Fourteenth, and went immediately to seek out Miss Dauntry and pass on the good news.

So it was not long before Catherine heard it also; although by this time she was distinctly too care-worn to rejoice with the other two. Of course, it *must* be good, she told herself, to be assured of leaving Challow and Mr Berrington so soon and for ever. If the dreaded pledge from him came within the next few hours, it would be easy for her to prevaricate over her answer until it was given to him—most effectively—tomorrow.

The constant forebodings which had afflicted her while she was in Kent had now taken their toll. She was sleeping badly, had an indifferent appetite, and, all-round, was beginning to draw interested looks upon her from Aunt Wilby; always alert for signs of indisposition in her ward. Part of the strain she suffered stemmed from guilt that she would be deserting her kindly aunt and leaving her to face Lord Ebford's wrath alone. However, she knew it served no purpose to dwell on such secondary matters: she must think only of her future, and face it with the same determined resolution as dear Ben had shown. If only she were leaving here to join him, most of her anxieties would fall away, she reflected sadly.

Her thoughts were soon concentrated by the practical problems confronting her; even during their visit later that day to the Stoke's delightful family, she spent much of her time at the manor in calculating how she would be able to smuggle a portmanteau into the barouche. Luckily Mr Berrington appeared subdued, and disinclined to pay her particular attention, and when she learned that her aunt was to be taken next day on a tour of the Challow neighbours by no less than Miss Berrington herself, her mental burden was eased considerably. Rosalind, for her part, could scarcely restrain her cheerfulness when she realized that Lucian had not banned the expedition after all: this made it clear to her that in spite of his brave words he had evidently come to his senses at last, and was resigned to letting the girl go.

So one last night—almost devoid of slumber—had

to be endured by Catherine in her suitor's house. Then the moment came when, with great apprehension, she set off with her haphazardly packed valise down to the stables.

The long night had yielded a hundred ingenious ways of explaining this act to those who might bar her way; but no one did. Relief overwhelmed her—only to be at once dispelled, as she entered the stable building, by the sight of the bulky coachman standing squarely in her path. She had not bethought her at all of what *he* might have to say! She beheld him wild-eyed, as though he were an apparition.

But the perfectly ordinary servant advanced upon her with no horrid rattling of chains whatsoever, only a merry smile and the civil inquiry: "This goes in the barouche, Miss, I take it?" And he eased the bag from her rigid grasp.

Weak with relief, she managed to murmur her thanks and then set off back to the house before any more pertinent questions occurred to him. When she returned there, her aunt had already left for the round of duty calls with her hostess. Of Lucian Berrington there was no sign: after partaking of an exceptionally early breakfast it appeared he was keeping his room; so there was to be no last harrowing scene with him. Chattering away with Felix and Melissa a little later, her spirits at last rose, and she permitted herself to believe that all might go off successfully.

And so very shortly she found herself on the turnpike road to Maidstone. Letting her companions' constant talk—much of it in coy-sounding French—wash over her, she settled to her own thoughts as the vehicle rolled along.

She was finally forced to own to herself that Christopher had failed her. She still believed that he was fond of her; but not fond enough to do what he had promised. As she would now be staying for a while with one of his relations, their paths might well re-cross; but his indifference to her fate once she had left town was something which would always come between them.

But she could not find it in her heart to blame him: to triumph over the circumstances in which they found themselves would have demanded from him an order of spirited defiance, and disregard for the conventions, which he simply did not possess. In truth, until the moment when she actually stepped into the carriage, she had not been at all certain whether she had those qualities herself.

THIRTEEN

On that fateful day even the elements seemed inclined to favour Catherine's cause: the warm sunny spell having given way to a cloudy morning with a distinct chill in the air, she had been granted a plausible reason to don her blue velvet pelisse and carry an India shawl against any showers; instead of both bulky garments adding to the congestion in her portmanteau.

The same threatening weather persisted when Maidstone was reached. As the barouche turned off the main street and under a square-arched entrance, Melissa craned her head to look around the hood. "Some inn or other," she reported vaguely in a whisper. "The yard is small—this cannot be where the accommodation coach will take you up."

Nevertheless it was a bustling place, crowded

and alive with people, horses and a variety of carriages. As their own stately but rather old-fashioned vehicle halted on its ponderous springs, Catherine looked about in rising agitation, wishful that she had acquired just a little prior experience of public travel. She had tried to discuss earlier with Melissa what her next moves should be, but had met with a certain studied indifference. Having advanced her friend's escape plan thus far, Melissa was now perhaps disinclined for further personal involvement in it. Catherine understood this sentiment on her part, and indeed she was now anxious to proceed unaided, but common-sense seemed to indicate that she did nothing precipitate until it was too late for Mr Frodsham to become alarmed about her—and perhaps spoil everything.

No sooner had the three of them stepped down into the yard than the weather once again came to her assistance. A few spots of rain fell, developing into a light shower. Mr Frodsham was at once all concern, guiding his charges over to the shelter of the immediate hostelry, where, Catherine hoped, at least she might be able to discover the departure time and place of the public coach.

Felix, who was himself dressed point-device that morning, was gratified to be seen in the company of two such *élégantes*, who, as he was fastidiously aware, would not have disgraced him were he now in Rotten Row instead of this little market town. He accompanied them with great punctilio into the dining-room.

Busy though he was, the sharp-eyed landlord was instantly at their command, leaving their fellow-citizens in the random care of two overworked and rather decrepit waiters. Beer and lemonade were bespoken, and an offer of a strawberry flan overbore Miss Dauntry's resistance; but Catherine shook her head. Her appetite was quite gone now as the moment of decision beckoned to her.

When the landlord had left them Felix said drawlingly: "Well *mes enfants,* now that you have gulled me here to sit amongst these wool gatherers —or whatever they are—perhaps you will tell me how we are to amuse ourselves if this rain should persist?"

"Rain or no rain, I must slip out and make my purchases," Catherine announced a shade too loudly.

Felix blinked. "No, not the thing——" he began, but Melissa swiftly interposed:

"Oh, Cathy, you and your private buying! Poor Felix—he will have to cose for a while with his *choix secondaire.*"

This speech, and the dimpling smile which accompanied it, appeared to give him pause for reflection, but Catherine could see that he was still far from easy that she should leave the inn unattended. At this juncture, however, the landlord reappeared at their table, bearing not the expected refreshments but a message. "Sir, your coachman begs a word in the stable, if you please. I'll conduct you myself."

Felix rose with an impatient sigh; though secretly relieved that horse matters, rather than points of propriety, now needed his attention. Then, much struck, he said: "By God, if there should be something badly amiss with Berrington's roans. . . !" He hurried after the landlord.

"Well—here is your chance," Melissa said throbbingly.

Catherine's grip tightened on the reticule containing the twenty precious guineas that were all she had; unless she counted Melly's note of introduction to her cousin. "Oh, yes, I suppose so." She stared about the crowded, indifferent room with mounting desperation. "I still have to retrieve my valise from the carriage: how do you think——?"

"Clearly you can't do that now, but you can make inquiries about the coach. Oh, do *hurry,* or he'll be back! Even I cannot cozen him for ever if you keep *muffing everything!*"

At that reproach Catherine rose precipitately, and made her way blindly to the door. Her mind was still confused as to what she was to do. The first person she saw—or, rather, bumped into—was the landlord, come back from directing Felix.

"Beg pardon, ma'am," he murmured, eyeing her, she fancied, a little strangely. "I shall attend you with the order in just one moment."

"No, no, it isn't that." She hesitated, then blurted: "I wonder if you could inform me when the next coach to Bromley will pass through the town?"

A certain reserve settled over his friendly features. "You aren't meaning the *stagecoach,* ma'am? Not the common rumble?"

"Yes. There is one due, is there not?" She fought to keep the note of panic from her voice.

"To be sure there is, at three o'clock—but it's boarded at the Bull, they go in for that trade at the Bull," he told her with professional disparagement.

"You see, I have to put my—my maid safely on to it," she said with a burst of inspiration. His manner at once unstiffened, and he obliged her with the fullest information. "Thank you—thank you very much," she said effusively, her one thought now being to return to the table before Felix. And within the next few seconds she had stammered out the news to Melissa. "But, Melly, shall we still *be* in Maidstone by three?" she asked in an other onset of doubt.

"Of course, widgeon! I'll ensure that Felix promenades over every inch of this lamentable settlement, even if it is pouring."

"Oh, no, not in his fine clothes!" she cried inconsequentially.

"*My* clothes don't signify, I collect! There is something *selfish* about you Cathy, was you aware of that? Well, I shall disregard it for your sake. . . . Felix does not yet know that I am *very* religious: I shall insist upon seeing the church—for you know there is always at least one church that is considered worth going in, for some odd reason, even in the meanest place, which I am very sure this is!"

"Of course I'm obliged for all your kindness," Catherine murmured. "I can remain with you until half-past two and then I must make my way to the Bull. What will you tell Felix then?"

Melissa pouted. "The truth—well, a part of it: that you've gone off to call on an ailing aunt nearby—no, I shan't say where—and that I have an explanatory letter from you to deliver into the Colonel's hands. That should serve to hold up any search being launched until you are well clear."

"Yes, that sounds most ingenious." She refused to let herself think of how small a part in fact the truth had played in it. "Oh, do you think I *should* have written to Mr Berrington?"

"No—for you would only have muffed that too! I will pitch him the same tale as Felix, only without mention of a letter. Pluck up! You know you can depend on me to fend him off. . . . Here comes Felix now," she continued *sotto voce*. "We must be prepared for impromptu action if necessary." Her eyes were brimming with mischief, but Catherine was at least relieved to see that she was being everything that was helpful once again.

There was a certain air of harassment in their escort when he re-joined them. "What's amiss?" Catherine asked him, fearing now that such tentative plans as she had were about to be thrown into total disarray by matters outside her control.

"Eh? Nothing!—nothing at all—save only that I omitted to tell Simon when we intend returning to Challow."

His tone sounded forced, but all Catherine was concerned with was the time he had now set with the coachman, and she asked him this at once.

"We all fixed for——" He cleared his throat and began again: "I reckon about half-past three, if that suits?"

She sighed with relief: that would allow her ample time to be aboard the coach before Felix and Melissa returned to the inn from their protracted walk.

Felix was now saying: "I told the fellow he could take himself off for a heavy wet until then."

This remark afforded her further solace; the barouche would be left unattended, which removed the last nagging doubt from her mind over retrieving her portmanteau. Altogether she was now sanguine enough to feel able to do some justice to a slice of strawberry flan, when the landlord finally brought it.

They lingered at the inn for some little while until the rain cleared, then sallied forth to explore. It did not take very long to discover that the town's attractions were confined largely to one humble street descending to the river, where the only shops were to be found. In some of these Catherine made a great piece of work of not being able to decide upon her aunt's gift. The ultimate choice, she told the other two, lay between a pair of kid gloves obtainable at the top of the hill, and a pink cornelian brooch on offer down near the Medway. As the crucial hour approached, finding them upon the higher ground, she declared that she would have the brooch after all; as it was now at the far end of the town she would meet them later at the inn.

Felix entered a plaintive caveat upon hearing this arrangement; but fortunately his legs had felt all the climbing, and he did not really wish to descend the hill until they felt more like flesh and bone again. In any case, he was promptly brought to heel by Melissa.

"Fiddlesticks!" she told him, right on cue. "You and I shall take the chance of walking over the church—it's up there, I collect. I have wanted to see it this age, you know, for it is one of the stopping places on the Pilgrims Way."

Felix groaned audibly; then raised his fair brows in surprise. "Forgive me—but surely you mistake?"

"I do not! The Pilgrims Way, from Winchester to Canterbury, does indeed—*must*—pass through here." Seeing that he remained sceptical, she reddened, but added in her firmest voice: "I believe the church is a particularly fine example of—of its kind, and in any event I should very much like to see it, *if* you please!"

"Do, pray, oblige her, Mr Frodsham," Catherine added her voice; while feeling intensely sorry for him. "I know how disappointed she will be else. I'm persuaded you need have no qualms for my safety in such a sleepy little place as this."

"If you say so, ma'am," Felix gave way with a helpless shrug. He still appeared bemused by Miss Dauntry's unlikely passion for ecclesiastical architecture. Showing no similar fervour he began plodding after her up the hillside.

Catherine set forth at a steady pace towards the inn they had visited. Once there, she had the good fortune to find a helpful lad who lifted her bag down from the barouche, then readily consented to carry it for her to the Bull.

The yard of the Bull was much larger than that of the other inn, with two private carriages waiting there upon the expanse of cobbles and also a yellow post-chaise in process of having its horses changed. Several persons stood about, but Catherine did not care to approach any of them with the several unanswered questions that were still clamorous in her head. It seemed clear that most of them were waiting to board or meet the coach, and so she paid off the boy and took up a place a little apart from the others under the wooden gallery.

The coach came early; for only minutes later, and before she had had time to grow too agitated, the guard's bugle sounded and then almost at once a coach-and-six drew up with a flourish in the yard; which all of a sudden appeared small and over-crowded. She saw there were a dozen or so cramped-looking souls aboard the roof, which made her fearful that she might be forced to occupy an outside seat herself.

Ostlers were soon nimbly detaching the animals, and a few travellers clambered from their high perch, but the coach steps were not let down and its doors remained shut. The guard, approached in line by the hopeful new passengers, was checking them off against a list in his hand. In no time at all the vacated outside seats were claimed, and Catherine realized with stark horror that there were no others available to her. "Please, please, I wish to go to Bromley!" she shouted beseechingly to the guard above the hubbub.

He frowned at her from under his broad-brimmed hat, and then back at his list. "You ain't booked on, are you, pretty one? 'Cause the way-bill's made right up for this time—'less you fancies a ride with Tiny Liza!" He broke into a cackle, and jerked a thumb towards the basket slung at the rear of the coach. There, Catherine's appalled gaze encountered the largest and most unkempt woman she had ever seen: clutched to her vast bosom was a chicken, and at the end of a frayed rope two vociferous piglets rooted about in the miscellaneous baggage surrounding their sow-like owner.

This Hogarthian scene served both to rivet and absorb her attention, and before she knew it the stage had suddenly jolted on its way without her. Her throat tightened, and sickness churned inside her. She seemed rooted to the spot, and a voice beside her had to repeat its opening address before she returned, dazedly, to her present awful situation.

"Forgive me, my dear, but I could not but divine that your attempt to go to Bromley was, ah, frustrated. You would do me a great honour if you would permit me to put my chaise at your disposal."

She looked up to regard a tall, middle-aged and rather overfashionably attired gentleman at her side. His demeanour was assured, and his expression was one of deep concern for her plight. However, tyro that she was in the ways of public travel, she did know that a single lady could not hire a post-chaise on her own account; and certainly she could not share such an equipage with a man.

Summoning a shred of dignity, she faltered: "It is kind in you, sir, but out of the question for me to take advantage of such an offer." She waited for his bold expression to change, but when it did not she searched desperately in her mind for some incontrovertible reason, outside of obvious propriety, why this should be so. "My—my brother will be here betimes to take me h–home." Her lips trembled upon that last word, for now it had become the most painful one in all her vocabulary. "He told me he would, in case—in case there should be no seat for me on the coach."

"Come, you don't expect me to swallow that," the stranger said with a certain unpleasant impatience. "For if *any such* relation was so solicitous for your welfare, he would most assuredly not permit you to travel without a maid—or, for that matter, to take the common stage in all that, ah, finery."

She blushed as he surveyed her in a knowing manner; and then her embarrassment increased to real alarm as his insolent gaze rested upon the reticule containing all her money, still gripped in her hand after her attempt to buy a ticket. The yard had become quickly and frighteningly deserted now that the stage was gone, with only one private carriage left standing there. She contemplated the latter with growing consciousness and fear.

"Yes, that's mine! A prime little turn-out, eh, my angel?" he murmured, noting the direction of her glance. "And, I'll dare swear, vastly more comfortable than any, ah, conveyance for the populace. Damme if I ain't intrigued how one of your, ah, *sweet appearance* must needs travel by such means! But come and look it over for yourself!"

He smiled at her for the first time, and she saw with a kind of stricken fascination that some careful maquillage on his face was now cracking about his eyes. By the time she had recovered from her revulsion at this sight, he had calmly picked up her portmanteau and was walking away with it towards the solitary vehicle.

Really frightened now, she chased after him and seized hold of the valise to try and wrest it from him. But his muscles seemed distinctly better preserved than his features: his grip was like iron and quite immovable, until, without warning, he switched the bag from one hand to the other and simultaneously she found her own hand painfully imprisoned in his. In spite of her frantic efforts to break free, they proceeded inexorably towards his carriage.

Once alongside it, he tossed down the portmanteau and, with both those powerful arms free from encumbrance, met with not the slightest difficulty in bundling her into the rocking chaise. As soon as she perceived that he was trying to shut her in she grasped the door by its frame and braced with all her might against it, desperation lending her more than her usual strength; and, as if from someone else's body, she heard a long thin scream coming from out her own lungs.

It darted through her brain that if she could only delay him, some rescuer must surely answer that cry and appear in the yard. But he still held the door closed with apparent ease, and was stooping to fasten it in some way when all at once she heard him choke; then the door flew suddenly open and banged backed against the panel of the chaise; whereupon she pitched forward from the vehicle and fell on to the rough stones.

In her dazed condition her first and only concern, before she attempted to stand up, was for the dropped reticule containing her money and her letter of introduction to Henrietta Oaks, but as she groped about the cobbles she became aware of two pairs of stamping top-booted legs, only a short distance away from her. There was also the sound of blows, and hard breaths, above her head, as she espied her reticule and snatched it up. Only then did she waver unsteadily to her feet.

As she did so, she was in time to see her would-be abductor assuming a horizontal position himself; and his triumphant assailant rushed towards her. She gave a further little cry of fear, but was now so feeble it scarcely sounded. Helplessly she waited for this new villain to take her, or her possessions, or both.

"Catherine!—oh my love, are you hurt?"

When she saw it was Mr Berrington she did not know whether to run away, or stay her ground. In the event, though, no such choice had to be made, for his arms were about her and he was still inquiring, in the most distracted tones, if she had sustained any injuries.

"No, no!" she said in a breaking voice into his shoulder, and unaware of precisely what it was that she was denying with such vehemence.

His arm tightened gently round her waist and he moved her more upright, saying: "Do you feel able to walk into the inn? You will not be long observed, there is a private parlour at your disposal."

By now she was shaking with nerves and bereft of speech, and knowing herself to be right on the edge of shedding a whole lake of tears on to the drab coat of her rejected suitor. She managed to nod, and he guided her forward in silence until they were inside the hostelry. There, he managed in some incalculable way to shield her from a host of vulgar inquisitive eyes while helping her to the top of a pair of stairs leading off the tap-room, which had been the nearest entrance on to the yard.

He opened the door of a small apartment by the stairhead. "I will send in the chambermaid to you—and when you feel sufficiently well, come down to the coffee room." And, with a stiff little bow he left her.

When the maid arrived, several minutes later, she was still standing in a trance-like state in the middle of the parlour. The servant had come well-prepared, being laden with a basin, a jug of hot water, a wash-ball, a linen towel and a clothes brush. Evidently possessing a temperament quit unattuned to high drama, she announced cheerfully: "There now, miss, if you'll take off that bonnet and pelisse I'll do what I can to restore them for you, only no promises!"

Catherine stared at her and then slowly down at her clothes. "Yes," she said blankly, "they are muddied, thank you." She wondered what tale Mr Berrington had told them below to account for her shocking appearance; then shook her head, apprehending that it was not his character to tell anyone tales, ever. She gave a loud sniff, but the phlegmatic chambermaid seemed not to notice.

In the quarter-hour or so which it took the experienced inn-servant to render her more presentable, she slowly made a recover from the double shock of being molested by one man and then saved by another—from whom she had been doin her utmost to escape. The bitter irony of it was not lost on her, but she was entirely baffled how it had come about. The thought of now having to explain to him downstairs made her sink; but the notion of a further attempt at flight made her sink still more; and besides, she just could not treat him so after such gallantry and forbearance. No, the time had now clearly come when she must at last speak out.

Dismissing the maid, she drew a comb through her wilting brown waves and tucked them under her bedraggled straw bonnet. Then, taking a deep breath, she went downstairs.

Lucian was at her side as soon as she crossed the threshold of the coffee room. His face still showed no anger, only relief as he said to her:

"Were you greatly shaken by that experience?—no, that's an idiotic question! Of course you were—and we shall stay here quietly for a while until you feel able to face the others again." He seated her beside him at a little table.

"The others?" she repeated, frowning. Apart from the two of them she had forgotten all others.

"Yes, Felix and Miss Dauntry will still be waiting at—what's it called?—the other inn, to travel back with you."

"But what time is it?"

"Not much gone three, so you won't delay them unduly."

She lifted her eyes to him directly for the first time since her rescue. "You knew all our—arrangements, then?"

He sighed. "Yes, I think so."

"Oh." And as she considered the implications of this short exchange, there did not seem much else she could add to it; but, after an interminable silence, she forced out: "I'm sorry, I haven't thanked you for putting that beastly man to flight. I don't know how I should have fared without you." It struck her then that these words were not well-chosen as a preliminary to telling him she couldn't marry him; but nevertheless they came from her heart.

"I'm only glad I was there in time," he said formally, as the waiter leaned over them with refreshments. "You will take some tea?"

But that neutral question dealt a final blow to Catherine's ravaged nerves. That he should have noticed that this beverage, customarily served only after dinner, was her favourite at all times, and that he had especially ordered it now, quite broke her spirit. She put her face in her hands and wept.

He waved the waiter off, then poured some of the affecting drink into a cup and pushed it gently towards her.

"Thank you," she whispered, still snuffling in a manner which she knew must only give him a further disgust of her, "I'm sorry for—so sorry. . . ."

He regarded her with infinite sadness. "No, it is I who am sorry that you should have been driven to such lengths. And I wish you to know you may rest easy that I shall persist no longer in my—my great ambition to make you my wife. Had you succeeded in boarding the stage in safety I wouldn't have interfered, but merely——" He broke off, preferring to leave unsaid his original plan of following on horseback at a discreet distance to ensure she came to no harm while en route. "Now," he continued in more prosaic accents, "drink your tea and I will take you back to your friends. I told Felix not to regard it if you were a trifle late, but we don't want to rouse his curiosity too much, do we?"

FOURTEEN

It was not Felix's curiosity, so much, which needed to be allayed when Catherine returned to them at the smaller inn, but that of Melissa.

For ever since Lucian had summoned his hapless nephew to the stables earlier, under the guise of the message from Simon-coachman, Felix had been a trifle confused; Catherine's eventual reappearance did not add significantly to that condition.

He had, of course, been most willing to do as he was bid and relinquished responsibility for Miss Ebford to his uncle from that point on; understanding, if only vaguely, that he was required to make a show of concern if the young lady should propose to walk about the town unaccompanied, but that he was in no way to attempt to constrain her. Had he been consulted as to his own view of these proceedings, he would have felt bound to say that it all seemed devilish smoky. Why Lucian should go to such lengths to set up a clandestine meeting with one of his own guests, he couldn't fathom; unless it was to avoid the scrutiny of that ape-leader sister of his. But he was not asked what he thought. Instead, Lucian had spoken a few pointed words to him concerning his Paris visit, after which the young gentleman had hastened to reassure him that he was at his command in all things.

And so, not surprisingly, Melissa had been quite unsuccessful in persuading him that Catherine would not be returning to Challow. Vehement in this opinion though she was, he was more inclined to believe what Lucian had told him upon this head: that the girl would be going back with them unless he personally informed him otherwise. Felix's unpliant attitude had caused Melissa's frustration to mount considerably as they continued to sit and wait, until, to her stupefaction, Catherine walked in.

By then, her sad suitor was already riding homewards, having left it to her to account for her absence to the pair of them as best she might.

"*Cathy!* For pity's sake! What has happened? You must have muffed it! You look awful!" Melissa greeted her.

"Oh, devil a bit, she'll pass," said Felix. It now only remained for him to convey the two of them safely back to Challow, and Lucian had warned him that Miss Ebford might be agitated. Admittedly he had said nothing of her looking like a mudlark besides, but the whole affair had him grassed by this time, and he was determined to make the best of it. "Bound to get a bit besplattered after a shower of rain, you know," he observed heartily.

Melissa, ignoring this irrelevance, fixed Catherine with a look of wide-eyed inquiry. But Catherine could only shake her head in a warning fashion. She apologized to them for her tardiness and then suggested, to Melissa's further amazement, that they should set off back to Challow at once. Felix rose with alacrity; but then she remembered her abandoned portmanteau at the Bull. However, a moment's rueful thought reminded her that since Mr Berrington had anticipated and overseen her every stupid move that day, doubtless he had dealt with that matter in as efficient a way as with everything else.

An uneasy silence prevailed between the ex-conspiritors, relieved only by Mr Frodsham's unappreciated attempts to be civil, until the carriage was finally halted again beside the heraldic beasts which flanked the stone steps at Challow. Then, as they began the weary ascent to the entrance, Melissa sought to take her friend out of Felix's hearing. But the simultaneous appearance of their host in the portico above was clearly going to frustrate her even now, and she whispered in a rush: "Cathy, you *must* tell me what is happening or I shall burst! It is too, too bad of you! Whyever have you come back after *all we arranged?*"

"Don't fret—all is well now," Catherine told her with an odd fugitive smile. "I am not to be compelled to wed Mr Berrington, despite how it seemed."

This intelligence served to halt Melissa's climb abruptly. "But—but how is this?" Meeting with no further elucidation, she transferred her wide-eyed gaze to the figure of Lucian, now hurrying down to them.

Catherine murmured: "I'll explain later, Melly, I promise." Then she too turned all her attention upon Lucian, who, she noted, had not yet put off his riding clothes.

Joining them, he said with icy composure to Melissa: "Your obedient, ma'am—I trust you have spent an enjoyable day?" Catherine received a quick, careful smile. To Felix he merely nodded; a comprehensive gesture which managed to convey thanks together with other meanings, and which caused the young man to beam broadly.

Little of this escaped Melissa's now very heightened powers of observation, but matters were still not a whit clearer to her. And when, on their entering the house, Mr Berrington swept her friend into the small salon in the most solicitous style imaginable, she could only gape after them and draw the conclusion that everyone apart from herself had run mad.

Catherine was soon to suspect the very same thing after the next few minutes with her erstwhile suitor and rescuer.

Lucian inquired after her health, saw her placed in the most comfortable chair, and then drew aside a little with a certain awkwardness. He began pacing to and fro, occasionally casting somewhat haggard glances in her direction, though not precisely at her. Once he cleared his throat, but still hesitated on the brink of speech.

Unable to bear this, she said: "Mr Berrington, if you want to ring a peal over my head I wish you will do so! I have behaved abominably, and readily own to it."

He looked startled. "No!—dear me, no! As if I should commit such a gross injustice! If I seem—it is merely that I would have spared you this ordeal, today of all days, if it were in my power to do so—but I fear it is not."

She stared back at him in alarm, thinking that some ill-tidings had come to Challow during her nonsensical absence. Her thoughts inevitably flew to Ben. "Then tell me, sir, I beg you," she said quietly, feeling her heart speed its beat.

"I found some visitors awaiting me on my return," he began tentatively.

"Lord Ebford!" Catherine exclaimed, sure it must be he. "Oh, I cannot see him now!"

"No, it is not his lordship—tho' pray don't distress yourself on that quite *unnecessary* head. I will myself inform him of the—er—change of plan, and will ensure he lays no blame for it at your door."

"Thank you," she told him in the most heartfelt fashion. "You are everything that is kind, and I don't for one moment deserve it."

A look of pain crossed his features, but he continued smoothly: "We are forgetting the visitors—your visitors. Mr Christopher Dauntry is one of them."

Her hand jerked to her mouth. *"Christopher? Oh, no!"* So if only she had waited a little longer he would not have failed her after all!

"He has with him another—gentleman, known by the name of Robert Barton."

She frowned through some fresh tears in her

eyes. "Who is he? And why do you say 'known by'?"

"Because he claims to be someone quite else—Ebford's brother, in fact."

"But that cannot be," she said slowly. "He was never used to speak of any close kinsman."

"If this Mr Barton's story is true, that is not altogether strange," he said dryly.

Again she drew her brows together, "And what story is that, sir?"

"One that is most certainly not mine to tell. I think perhaps you should hear it from Mr Dauntry's lips—and then matters can perhaps be settled between you for your future—in every way," he concluded with a twitch of a smile which brought heat rushing to her face.

He suspected, then, that Christopher had come to snatch her away: perhaps Chris had told him that already. Were it possible, she felt still more uncomfortable in his presence, and to be discovering still greater depths of compassion and understanding in him. She hung her head, wishing, almost, that he *had* given her a Juniper lecture rather than this further degree of remorse.

Observing her, he said in a neutral way: "Tho' I daresay you might like to change first before meeting anyone?"

She gave a faint grimace, thinking of the barrage of questions awaiting her upstairs from Melissa; or her aunt. "No. Where is Mrs Wilby? Has she seen the visitors?"

"I think not. I believe she is with my sister in her boudoir, and perhaps it is best that she should remain in ignorance of Mr Barton's existence for the moment, I rather fancy. Now, shall I send Mr

Dauntry to you while I entertain Ebford's mysterious connexion?"

"Yes, if you please." Then she addressed his back in an almost inaudible tone: "I am vastly sorry to have drawn down all this uproar upon you—it makes me *twice* unforgivable in one dreadful day."

He shrugged, and before turning towards the door he favoured her with that potent species of smile to which she had become accustomed during her time in Kent; but now this must be the last occasion on which she would see it. "Oh, by the bye," he said thoughtfully, his hand on the door knob, "you must make up your own mind as to Barton and his claims. But there: I scarcely need indulge such qualms on your behalf, need I? Your independence of mind is proven to me beyond any doubt."

By the time this shaft had found its mark she was alone. Slowly she put off her soiled bonnet and pelisse, then delved into the still intact clutch of guineas in her reticule and finally drew out her comb. There was no looking-glass to consult, and in any case she was too weary in spirit to pay more than token heed to her appearance. After a few cursory strokes and pats at her hair she abandoned the attempt and crossed to the window, staring sightlessly outside until Christopher came.

She supposed he would know nothing of her abortive design to quit Challow, and feel no conscience on that head; whereas her own conscience was uneasy that she had not waited long enough for him to rescue her. It was an odd situation!

She spun round when the door clicked and they

greeted each other simultaneously. Christopher then took the initiative by saying: "First, I must tender my apologies—I've let almost a sennight pass without fulfilling my promise."

"Please, I don't regard that—I knew you would keep your word," she lied brightly.

He looked relieved, though, being acutely aware of how near he had been to failing her, still sought to justify himself. "Well, Cathy, it was perhaps a fortuitous delay, in the event, for if I had left town any earlier I would not have met Mr Barton." He paused portentously.

"Is he really Lord Ebford's brother?" she asked, pleased to turn to a subject which she supposed was not of great concern to either of them. "Why have you brought him here?"

Christopher then staunchly embarked upon the uneviable task of telling her that she had been the victim of a deception all her life. She listened to his quiet, unemotional voice relating these incredible things, and, despite everything that had happened lately, she could not help but be glad he had been the one to tell her this. When he had finished she gazed at him intently and said: "Do *you* believe him Chris?"

"Yes, I'm inclined to think he is telling the truth—in part because he does have a look of your brother about the features."

"Ah, dear Ben!" she exclaimed fondly. "Would that he were here instead of him!"

"Mr Barton is quite set upon discovering his whereabouts, he says—even if he has to go to the ends of the earth."

Her eyes lit up. "Is he, truly? Oh, bless him! *I*

am more than half inclined to believe anyone who would do such a splendid thing. What is he like?"

Christopher's face assumed that look of banker-like prudence which she had seen many times on his father's. "You must form your own opinion, of course. I would class him myself as a likable rogue. Don't forget he abandoned you both, without so much as a backward glance, for more than fourteen years."

"Yes, that puzzles me, I confess—the fourteen years, I mean. I must have been four when he left and yet I remember nothing of him—or of my mother," she said sadly.

"Well, he became quite expansive about the past when we posted down, and I fancy your lack of memories may be accounted for by the fact he was from home—gaming, I collect—much of the time, and your mother being a victim of delicate health was compelled to leave you in the servant's hands."

"Poor creature . . . I wonder if there is a likeness of her in existence? I should so love to see one."

"You will have the opportunity to ask Barton. I own that possibility had not struck me: it would serve to substantiate his story, I suppose, if there were such."

"I am all impatience now to meet him—but would you think me very foolish if I asked you to be present?"

"Of course not, if that is your wish." He hesitated, seeming to brace himself for still more weighty duties. "Catherine—how do things stand here? I mean, between you and Berrington: has there been any formal declaration?"

"Oh no! I should have told you at once. As soon

as he was acquainted with my sentiments, he most properly withdrew his offer," she said in a rather small voice.

"Oh—I see." His countenance brightened. He had not been relishing the kind of interview which, with a man like Berrington, he knew must have brought a hornet's nest about his ears.

"Yes. I know everyone, including you, told me it would be so! I fear I've made sad work of it all."

"Shouldn't blame yourself," he mumbled uncomfortably. "All deuced difficult—very understandable."

They were still far from easy with each other, and this meeting, which Catherine had imagined so often during the past anguished week, was falling lamentably short of her expectations. She had seen herself running eagerly into the arms of her rescuer, and being clasped in his anxious embrace. However, in the actual circumstances she supposed it was scarcely wonderful if their reunion should be less than blithe; but when he coughed several times, following that with the single word *"Catherine . . ."* said in a rather choked tone of voice, it occurred to her that despite this unpromising beginning he was indeed about to propose to her.

Telling herself that she could not face such an important question on a day already made momentous for her, she laid a restraining hand on his sleeve. "Chris, should you mind terribly if we went straightway to see Mr Barton? You do understand?" She tried to convey her comprehension of what he had been about to say to her by a particular glance.

He let out a long breath, but immediately concurred. "By all means, we will go to him at once."

"How do I look?" she asked him. "You know, it is a curious sensation to be meeting one's parent after all these years!" She gave an edgy little laugh.

He smiled broadly for the first time. "You look charmingly, as ever. If he *is* your father, he ought to be transported for serving you as he has!—tho' I suppose, in a sense, he transported himself. Anyway, remember you can have nothing with which to reproach yourself in the whole affair."

Thus reassured, Catherine went with him to the circular withdrawing-room. Lucian was there pointing out some detail of the gilt plaster reliefs on the domed ceiling to the visitor, and from a view of their backs she saw that the two men were of a height, although the stranger was a heavier build altogether.

When they turned at her entrance, their appearance could not have differed more; the bald head and round, ruddy face of Mr Barton contrasting with Lucian's neat thatch of silver black hair, and the lean patrician cast of features beneath it.

It fell to him to assume the bizarre task of introducing the claimant father to his daughter, and the two stared mutely at each other. Catherine was dead white, and even the less sensitive Barton appeared stunned, and labouring under great emotion.

"Catherine, my *dearest girl!*" He took one of her hands as if it were porcelain, and held her at arms length. "Yes," he sighed at last. "You could be Grace come back again." His eyes filled and looked away.

"That was your wife, sir?" she asked, forcing herself to speak. She had no sense of recognition or kinship with this plain and blunt man, and felt wholly at a loss in face of such powerful *empressement*. And yet, *was* there perhaps a something of Benjamin about those deep-set eyes, and the curve of the nose, as Christopher had suggested?

"It was, it was." He released her hand and began to search about in his pockets. "I have this of her—carry it everywhere. Not first rate, you understand, so it proves nothing, but—Ah, here we are!" He drew a soft skin pouch from his waistcoat, slipped an oval minature into his palm and handed it to Catherine.

She saw that, as he said, it was not a painting of quality; but the very poorness of execution made her throat tighten. It eloquently bespoke the straitened circumstances which must have surrounded its commission. But the artist had possessed talent enough to catch the air of debility which hung about the sitter. She looked at the haunted blue eyes as long as she could bear to, and then turned the miniature over. On the back was inscribed 'Grace Crowther, 1794'.

"Just before we were spliced," Mr Barton explained with some diffidence. "It was painted for me, Catherine."

She gave it back to him, her heart too full for speech; she was guiltily aware that she felt a great deal more affinity for the inanimate picture than for what must surely be a living parent in front of her.

Mr Barton now passed the little portrait to Lucian; who, with Christopher, had been a silent onlooker of the affecting scene. Lucian raised his eyes from the portrait to his beloved and back again, striving, unsuccessfully, to be dispassionate. "Yes: I believe they favour to a degree— though 'tis deuced hard to pin-point. How say you, sir?" He handed it to Christopher.

That gentleman added his considered assent, remarking that Benjamin bore a more obvious resemblance to Mr Barton. The latter became the object of their still greater depth of scrutiny, until even his high colour was deepened by it.

"Could you not prove the case by reference to some record of the marriage?" Lucian said at last, in the most courteous tone he had yet addressed to him.

"Possibly—but even that wouldn't be incontrovertible proof that I *am* Robert Ebford, would it?" He spread out his large hands in a gesture of helplessness. "Any road, if Catherine herself believes, that is all I want! Remember, all of you, I'm not over here to turn my own skeleton out of the cupboard! I'm fully content to have found her again. . . ." He bit his lip, and was silent.

"I daresay you'd prefer to be left with her for a while," Lucian said next. Catherine wanted to cry out *'No!'* shrinking from any such *tête-à-tête,* but he himself replied.

"I think not, Mr Berrington—there's no hurry, after all. Cathy and I can make each other's acquaintance by stages, after I take her away from here." A certain firmness had now entered his former humble demeanour, and he cast a somewhat challenging glance at his host at this point.

Christopher emitted some faint spluttering

sounds of embarrassment at what he knew to be Barton's moralistic determination to employ force, if necessary, to remove Catherine from her suitor's— or seducer's—house. Unfortunately he had found no opportunity to tell him that such a drastic procedure need no longer be resorted to.

However, Lucian soon set all anxieties at rest by blandly according to the proposal. ". . . But I trust you will not feel compelled to set forth this instant. Miss Ebford has had a wearisome and tiring day already, and I cannot think she would wish to undergo the exigencies of a further journey, however short. So, my dear sir, I shall be more than delighted if you, and Mr Dauntry, will consider yourselves my guests, at least until the morning."

For some curious reason, however, this skilful diplomacy did not allay Catherine's apprehensions. Rather, it served to sharpen her senses and bring her true feelings into sudden and positive focus. She looked at the burly adventurer who said he was her father; then at the familiar face of Christopher, with its customary expression of pink and immature unease; and finally at Mr Berrington. She knew then, with a piercing clarity, that the very last thing she desired was to be parted from him. She had been so foolishly intent upon escape that she had been blind to the fact that her love and respect for him had been growing all this while. But now the strength of that realization was such that it threatened to deprive her of breath, and she had to make an immense effort to answer before Mr Barton could. "No, I cannot!" she cried loudly.

"Then of course you need not, my dear." Mr

Barton had been disarmed by his host's tractable response, and a swift and shrewd glance in Mr Dauntry's direction had informed him that, somehow, all was now well in that quarter. "We will gladly avail ourselves of Mr Berrington's kind hospitality over-night."

"No, that is not what I meant, sir." She was trembling violently, but knew she must speak out now or the chance would be lost to her forever. "I don't want to leave here tomorrow either. . . . Indeed, I would very much like to stay here for as long as Mr Berrington should ever wish!"

This declaration greatly affected those who heard it: Christopher opened and closed his mouth several times, looking rather like a freshly-caught hake; Robert Barton turned quite purple, and then burst out with some foreign-sounding expressions which she did not apprehend, but which were evidently indicative of his very strong indignation; while as for Lucian, he did not utter a word but merely searched his beloved's eyes, hardly daring to hope that the explanation he desired so much was to be found there.

She walked towards him, oblivious of her outraged parent, saying in a small, determined voice: "I would like to marry you, after—after all."

She stood before him like a penitent child, and, equally careless of their audience, he murmured: "My darling girl!", and embraced her.

Even Mr Barton was silenced by this turn of events. He cast a look of commiseration in Mr Dauntry's direction, surprising a broad smile upon that young gentleman's countenance, *Dammit, the young shaver looks pleased!* he thought, dumfounded all round at the behaviour of his erstwhile countrymen.

Lucian, who had just had the exquisite and wholly unforeseen happiness of seeing his fond smile at last returned by the one he loved, was for once at a loss for words. But Barton, after shaking his head a deal more over the situation, eventually found his voice again. "I guess it's time we took our leave, Dauntry," he said gruffly.

This served to bring Lucian back to the present with a jolt. "No—no, please, you must hold us excused! Truly," he went on with a boyish grin, "I hadn't the least suspicion that I was about to receive a proposal of marriage!" His arm remained about Catherine's waist as if he were afraid she might even now repent her decision. "It does occur to me, though," he continued, the laughter-lines gradually leaving his face, "that it might prove a shade awkward if Mr Barton were to come smash up against Mrs Wilby, as she is Lord Ebford's kinswoman. Don't you agree, my love, or am I being over-stuffish?" But she only nodded with great vigour at whatever he might choose to do, supremely content to let him order everything exactly as he pleased, either for that day or, indeed, for the duration of her life.

It was then settled between them that it would be for the best if Mr Barton should leave the house before dinner, but only after a private talk with Catherine. Christopher was to stay the night at Challow, and Lucian intimated to him with a degree of forcefulness that if he could escort his sister back to town the next day it would be appreciated.

Later, when Catherine was closeted with her

father, the new joy was still shining out of her eyes, and even he could see that there was no denying the situation. In any case, a little time for reflection had gone a great way to reconciling him to it. He much admired success, in all things; and who could deny that his daughter had made a most successful and impressive match? He had to own that Brother George had done her proud in that respect; even if he did seem to have been a touch maladroit in his handling of the affair, just as you'd expect of a stiff-rumped cove like George. But he was really delighted to see her so happy, and told her that he felt mightily privileged to have been present, against all the odds, at such a crucial point in her life.

"I call it handsome recompense, my child, for one who, God knows, has done naught to deserve it," he said humbly, and taking her hands in his he lifted them to his rough lips.

At that they both wept a little, each overwrought after a day of high emotions, but when calm reigned once more their thoughts turned inevitably to the missing member of the family. "I intend to find Ben, never fear, if it darn well takes me the rest of my days," he assured her. "It's the least I can do. Now, I've seen you're so well settled, it kind of makes it all the more important to find out what happened to your brother: I shan't rest till I know."

There was pitifully little Catherine could tell him by way of aiding him in his search. She showed him Ben's last letter, which she had kept hidden in the lining of her reticule.

"Lordy, now!" he cried out when he was reading it through. "The boy figured to go to the Land of

217

Opportunity! Now ain't that the strangest thing—almost as if he somehow knew—But no, that's sheer fancy, and I must be *practical* above all else." He frowned, and his bright eyes almost vanished behind their fleshy deep-set lids. "Start at the docks, that's the ticket! I might share another mutton chop with that pal of his from the Bank—Mr-Charlie Bone—and see if I can dig some more information out of him. I owe finding you to that young fellow, you know."

"I can well believe it, sir: Charlie was a good friend of Ben and of mine," she told him warmly.

"Well, I guess I should go now," he said presently, with a deep sigh. "However my quest for Ben turns out, I intend having this miniature of your mother copied in London. I'll contrive somehow to put it into your hands myself, and perhaps by then, who knows, there'll be some news of the boy."

There followed a fond parting which she would never have forseen only minutes ago, but, sustained by her new-found love for Lucian she was later able to face the rest of the company with calm composure.

Indeed, most of the others round the dinner table were markedly more agitated than she. Miss Berrington was in a state of shock which precluded even her customary bare civility; Melissa was very sulky, and professing total disbelief of what sparse—not to say maddening—intelligence as she had been able to extract from her deceitful trickster of a friend; Felix was still baffled by his uncle's antics but still hopefully indulgent, since his senses told him that Paris was now as good as in his grasp; and as for Honora Wilby, while naturally excited and pleased by the news she told herself that she had never really doubted that the girl would come to her senses in the end.

Only one present factor now served to mar Catherine's happiness to some degree: she felt that she had made heartless and disagreeable use of Christopher's feelings for her, and at the first opportunity after he came back to the drawing-room she sought a quiet word with him.

She had to own that he was bearing up very well under the blow. "Allow me to tender my very best wishes for your future," he said resonantly. "I collect you have made the right decision—even if it did take a little time," he concluded with his gentle smile.

"You are too kind to me!" she replied in some confusion. "I don't know what to say to you, Chris. I have gone on in the most monstrous fashion, I know—setting everyone in a bustle," she continued vaguely; unable to meet those ardent eyes of his which were yet so nobly innocent of reproach. "Can you ever forgive me?" she said tragically.

Christopher's cheeks glowed a more hectic shade still as he assured her: "There is naught to forgive, believe me! I, too, am at a loss, Cathy! You see, I intended to tell you earlier—just before we went in to meet your father—that I couldn't— wasn't free to——" He ran a finger around his wilting neck-cloth, and with more than a hint of anguish blurted: "In short, I've met someone else I hope to wed!"

Her huge astonishment dissolved promptly into the joy that was now never far away from her. "Oh, *Chris,* I can't express how happy I am for you!" Her voice rang out under the domed ceiling and several eyes stared across at them.

"Thank you—only pray don't breathe a word to a soul yet, I beg!" he pleaded, with a wild glance around the room and particularly in Melissa's direction. But he need not have alarmed himself in that quarter, Catherine observed with amusement; Miss Dauntry sat slumped and glazed-eyed, and quite beyond taking any interest in her brother's doings.

"Of course I shan't—it shall be our secret. May I know her name?"

"Well, in the ordinary way I wouldn't have spoken of it yet—it seems hardly the thing."

"*Please,* Chris, for what with—everything—I shan't be back in town this age, and by then you'll have proposed—and been accepted, depend on it!"

"Oh, very well, then—it is Lady Honley. I don't think you have met."

"No, I don't believe we have," she replied neutrally, but only to spare him further embarrassment over his disclosure. In fact she well recalled the golden-haired and sweet-faced young widow befriended by Lady Olivia. Thinking of her, while still looking at Christopher, it came to her that they were well suited.

Neither she nor Christopher was cognizant of the fact that her ladyship had intended the Countess not for him, but for Lord Ebford; and that every one of her match-making designs lay in ruins that evening, although she was still in happy ignorance of this. That ignorance was not to be preserved for very long: Melissa had listlessly agreed to return home on the morrow once she learned that Felix was leaving too, and could be

relied on to regale her mother with every detail of
the disastrous sojourn in Kent; also, Christopher,
galvanized by his indiscretion in speaking Lady
Honley's name, was to offer for her in the next
four-and-twenty hours, and receive a favourable
answer in rather less than that time; following
the combined strain of which events, Lady Olivia
would have urgent recourse to the Family Practi-
tioner, and be prescribed a nauseous draught and
prolonged period of bed-rest.

Lord Ebford's expectations, on the other hand,
were to be gratified. He soon received his invitation to the betrothal gathering at Challow, and it
served to banish from his mind any lingering
distaste occasioned by the visit from his reprobate
brother. It even put him more in charity with his
partner, William, in conjunction with the latter's
appearing to mend his ways of late regarding the
question of injudicious loans. Besides, he now felt
assured that with Berrington's backing made
certain, the Bank would be more than secure
against Dauntry's lapses.

But his complacency suffered a severe check
while he was still staying in the country.

By then the betrothal party was over and done
with. A certain lassitude overhung Challow and
its inhabitants on the day following, and Catherine, Mrs Wilby and Lord Ebford were taking their
ease on the Rose Terrace in company with Rosalind; who had mended her manners a trifle since
his lordship's arrival. Beyond their earlier visit to
morning service in the village church the party
had scarcely stirred in the July heat, but then
Machin came out to them to announce that Miss

Ebford was required to attend upon his master in the study.

Rosalind scowled, first at the butler for what she thought of as his premature deference to the chit, and then at Catherine herself as she rose to follow him. She was not a jot nearer to reconciliation with her brother's choice of bride, but had amended her earlier attitude to a positive looking forward to quitting Challow as soon as maybe, to set up her own establishment; and there to await, patiently, Lucian's Inevitable Disillusionment.

Catherine walked behind the servant, mischievously copying his rather flat-footed tread. She was still in something of a dream after scaling the dizzy heights of bliss at the assembly the night before, and when she stepped into Lucian's den it was a good half-minute before she saw there was someone with him, standing in the shadow. But then it was no time at all before she cried: *"Ben!"* and they were hugging each other, and laughing, with all their might.

Lucian looked on with quiet satisfaction, and giving silent thanks that this one flaw in his future wife's contentment was now removed. Then he slipped out of the room unnoticed to break the news to Ebford, and to do his best to dampen that individual's undoubted wrath over the penitent's return; except that Benjamin was not truly penitent at all, he suspected.

As Ben related his adventures over the past twelve months, Catherine gradually grew calmer. She reflected that he looked aged a good deal more than one year. She had seen him last a rebellious boy, and now here he was a sturdy, bronzed-faced man, dressed with no expense spared by the efficient Mr Barton. Time had also strengthened the resemblance to his father, and she finally accepted their relationship.

She listened enthralled as he told of how he had been tricked by the captain of a ship which he understood was bound for America. The scoundrel had taken his passage-money, but the gullible Ben had been forcibly put ashore at Dublin. Almost penniless, he had spent the whole of the intervening time seeking to earn enough to live on. She heard that had it not been for the generosity of a lady traveller, who had discerned that he was no ordinary link-boy, and who had paid his fare across the Irish Channel on the understanding that he returned home, he would have been in Ireland still.

Catherine herself was now a little older in the ways of the world, and conscious that perhaps there was something left unspecified in this interesting account. But she was far too delighted to be feasting her eyes on her dear, naughty Ben to be able to say a word of doubt to him.

"And so Mr—our father traced you at last?" she prompted when he at last paused for breath.

His teeth looked stronger and whiter than ever against the tanned face. "Yes: a great gun, is he not? We dealt famously, once Charlie brought us together. Of course, I looked up good old Charlie as soon as the ship got in."

They fell to discussing the incredible advent of a parent into their lives, and then Benjamin made a further revelation to her. "The thing is, Cath, he's asked me to go back to America with him. I've told him I will." He studied her face concernedly as she turned it away from him in shock. "Wish

223

me well—and, in any event, it won't happen until after the war is over."

"Are you quite sure you want this? You know, Lord Ebford might well forgive you, given time," she argued, without much conviction.

"Not he! Besides, Cath, I do desire to go—I'm sorry if that pains you."

"No—you must do whatever you feel is true to yourself," she said slowly. She was aware that this advice was ill-expressed, but nevertheless it seemed to sum up her own experience in life. She struggled to give better voice to it. "You are absolutely in the right to seize this opportunity. I was very nearly too idiotic to do so myself, you know, when it was offered to me, but tho' I don't in any degree deserve it I have been given my heart's desire. And it seems that now you have been granted yours, too, dearest Ben."